LAST DANCE AT THE END OF THE WORLD

Jacqueline Druga

Cover design by: Jacqueline Druga

Printed in the United States of America

A special thank you to Paula, Kira, and Wendi for all your help along with my Betas!

LAST DANCE
At the End of the World

Jacqueline Druga

ONE – LIFE NOW

August 3

If only.

If only I could go back and change my course. Instead of taking the path with life, what if I had chosen to die?

Death was a gift; one I had the option to take or leave behind.

Some would say I was fortunate to be able to choose what I was going to do when so many others, countless others, never had the option.

It wasn't given to them.

Unlike me, they didn't have a choice.

The phrase 'some would say' was a joke now.

'Some' would refer to many and there weren't many left to say anything.

Although to be fair, I didn't roam the countryside, my life wasn't a road trip. I didn't want to venture too far from my hometown, too far from my home.

It was all I had left.

My existence was centered there, our amazing two-story apartment above a storefront. I had made into an art gallery for my wife. A place to showcase her brilliant work and sometimes sell something. It didn't matter if she sold anything, that gallery meant the world to her. We bought the building, for what seemed like pennies. It was during the small town revitalization plan to make our Tennessee town look more storybook, or the way Hollywood would depict a small town. Bring in tourists! Whatever the reason, it was a steal.

We spent seven years making that building truly ours, along with every penny we had. Knocking down walls in the run down, upstairs apartments, we created a living space in our small town that could give any lavish New York apartment a run for its money.

The two, third-floor apartments would be homes for our children, should they need them when they became adults.

During the day I worked my printer job to pay the bills, at night I worked on our building.

My wife Maranda was a substitute teacher during the day, at night she created.

We had plans. Long term plans.

Then it all came to a screeching halt.

Maybe not as fast as it seemed, but it crashed down around our heads.

Nothing exploded, no wars, no alien invasion or dead beings ripping the living to shreds.

Our world, our bustling, beautiful, loud world … went out with a whimper.

The large living room of our home, once filled with laughter, love and clutter was now one big shrine of everything and anything I ever held dear.

Pictures, drawings, papers, graded homework assignments, anything and everything, covered every inch of the walls.

So, each day it was a reminder of a life I would never forget.

Like a lunatic, I wanted to remember every single thing.

While walking, or doing anything, I recited things out loud as reminders, *'Maranda loved old movies, Beau's third grade teacher was Mr. Richter. Daisy called me Daddy-Da. My mother smelled sweet, and my father drank Jack Daniels with a twist of lime'*

Things like that.

It was crazy in a good way.

My sanity was still intact, still strong, I made sure it stayed that way.

I hoped it was.

For a while there, I doubted it.

I lived in a mostly silent world; choosing who I talked to and when. The comforting noise was that which I created. My music, videos from my phone and tablet represented life.

Voices of all those I loved and would never hear again. The same voices which stopped talking long before they ever left me.

I was it. I was all that remained of my family.

Even though there were others, I felt like a lone survivor.

Maybe I am bound to live alone in my new existence?

An existence of my choice.

I made the choice to live. More so I chose 'memories', because for every single living being on the planet, the memories were the first to go.

I couldn't forget.

I owed the world that much.

TWO – A HINT IN THE AIR

February 3

SIX MONTHS EARLIER

“Travis, can you take this down to Dewalt’s?”

“Like, right now?” I asked.

“Yeah, if you can. They want to have these out a couple days ahead of the sale.”

“Don’t you think they should have planned for that?”

“Should have, could have, but come on man, you’re just giving me a hard time to give me a hard time.”

Connor Stevens was a good man. Same age as me, his kids were a little older than mine, but I had worked for him for nearly two decades.

What could I say? I wasn’t just a creature of habit; I was dedicated to a fault. If I found something I liked, I stuck with it. That included everything. From the food I ordered at restaurants, to the peanut butter we bought.

All the same. Never changing.

I was the exact same way at work. If I was working on something, I finished it. I set my mind to the schedule. If a date was set for an item to be delivered, that was the day it got there.

Changing up at the last minute was a small pet peeve of mine. Especially Dewalt’s, they did this all the time.

“Travis? The sales flyers are ready to go. Did you see them?”

“Nope.”

"Buy one pound, get one pound free on select deli meats."

"What the hell am I gonna do with all that deli meat?"

"Freeze half," said Connor.

"Oh, who the heck freezes lunch meat? Never tastes the same."

"Travis, take the box of flyers."

I grumbled. We were a five man operation, but our output was so high, we should have had ten. I was in the middle of packing the box with political postcards. "You aren't asking me because I am set to deliver these postcards to Mayor Todd, are you?"

"Not if you tell me you're not gonna give him a hard time."

"Fine. Let me finish this and I'll take the box," I said.

"You can finish them when you get back."

"No, I'll finish it now and put it in the truck. If I leave it, you'll have Jan finish and she'll take it because she loves Mayor Todd."

"Everyone does," he said.

"I don't."

"You don't because of silly reasons."

That made me laugh. "Silly? You're a grown ass man telling me I'm doing something silly."

"Travis, take the goddamn sales flyers." Connor stepped back and stopped, raising his eyebrows a few times. "How was that for grown up talk? Huh?"

"Very good."

"You're a strange man, Travis Grady."

Was I? Probably. But strange in a good way. I was a happy man, really, life was good to me. I wasn't one to complain.

Dewalt's was busy. It usually was midday. People would be out shopping, trying to get back home with the groceries before the kids got out of school. Dewalt's was a staple in our town of Loudon. I had gone to school with Eddie Dewalt. He ran the store. His father still owned it, but Eddie had really made it something. It used to be the store you went to for a few items or when a person didn't want to drive fifteen miles to the nearest Walmart. Now, it was the go to place.

We always shopped there.

I made a mental note to go before that big 'buy one, get one pound of deli meat' sale. People came from the next town for that.

It wasn't the good stuff. Usually the meat was left over, or stuff they had too much of. Still, it was a good deal if you liked deli meat.

There were four boxes of flyers, so I took them around to the back loading dock. It really wasn't much of a dock. A back entrance off the side street. Even the big delivery trucks couldn't fit back there, they had to drop off out front.

After loading the dolly, I carried the first three to the back, went back and got the fourth.

The stock guys were in the back. They all said hello and I asked if Eddie was in the office.

"Back office," one of the men answered. "Not front."

"Thanks." I carried the fourth box back to his office for Eddie to inspect.

His office was on the upper level. It had one of those windows to spy on the employees in the warehouse, but Eddie wasn't like that. His door was open, and I could hear the radio or something.

It was the news or sounded like it.

Balancing the box, I knocked on the partially open door.

Eddie was behind his desk, rocking back and forth as he stared at his computer.

"Hey," I called out.

"Oh." He turned in his chair some. "Hey, Travis, I didn't hear you."

"Obviously." I smiled. "I got your flyers for you. Early, too."

"Yeah." His eyes shifted to the computer.

"You know, Eddie, since you know you're having the big sale, why don't you put in the order for the flyers early?"

"Because I know it bothers you."

"Well, I need you to inspect them so I can drop off postcards for Mayor Todd."

"I don't know why he wastes his money," Eddie said. "He's gonna win."

"One day I'll beat him." I set the box on the desk and opened it. I noticed Eddie went back to watching his computer. Something definitely had his attention and it wasn't my presence with the flyers. I opened the flaps and pulled one out.

Pictures of bologna, ham and salami were on the front.

"How come you never have turkey on sale for the buy one, get one?" I asked.

"I'm sorry, what?"

"Never mind. So here you go," I said. "Take a look."

"Sure ... hey ... Travis ..." He sort of glanced at me, then went right back to his computer. "Didn't you have this?"

"Huh?" I was confused, standing there holding the flyer. "Have what?"

Eddie pointed to the computer and turned it slightly my way. "This virus."

I looked. Sure enough, Eddie was watching the news, the little ticker tape thing on the bottom read something about a virus.

"Is that a fake video on one of them sites or is that real news?" I asked.

"Real news. You had this right?" Eddie asked. "I mean, it was a big deal because it was rare, and you were like the town celebrity."

"Oh, yeah," I saw the name of the virus.

ARC.

When people hear the word 'virus' their mind goes to a cough, fever, rash, that sort of thing. Maybe even a stomach bug, but that wasn't what I had.

My first symptom was I forgot how to tie my shoes.

I mean, I really couldn't remember. I stared at my laces like they were some multilevel Rubik's cube.

It was rare and it had happened about three years or so earlier. I was one of about thirty people in our country, and the second in our state. They said there were more infected in Malaysia than the rest of the world combined, but it was still rare.

At first, I thought I had a brain tumor. Who at thirty-seven suddenly forgets how to tie their shoes? It worried me. Then I thought about my grandfather who had dementia. It was only when we went for test after test, my memory getting worse, that a lab technician taking my blood, brought up about something he had read online.

A virus carried by insects, something like Zika or Encephalitis.

Sure enough, I was later diagnosed with it. They never figured out how I caught it. They narrowed it down to this fishing trip. I didn't recall getting bit by a mosquito. Then again, my short term memory had started to decline.

I had a virus of the brain.

They called it the ARC virus.

Each person has the ARC gene, and ARC proteins.

It stood for Activity Regulator Cytoskeleton. Not that I was so smart to know that off the top of my head, but I had heard it so many times and read about it, it was embedded.

But learning the name for the acronym came after they cured it.

They cured it pretty fast, too. It took about seven months and I had that thing for the entire seven months. Medication kept me from getting worse. I wasn't as bad as some. I still couldn't remember how to tie my shoes even when my kids taught me. It was like a part of my brain was saying, 'no way, nope, not gonna learn'. But I still functioned, I went to work, Velcro shoes and all.

Something happened after I was cured, I started not only remembering, but I also had this memory that was impeccable. I didn't realize it had happened until they called me back for testing.

I was like super memory guy.

Boy, what I wouldn't have given to have that superpower in the tenth grade.

While the virus wreaked havoc for a brief period of time, the cure made the ARC gene stronger and the proteins powerful.

I didn't become the town celebrity because I had the virus, my fame was because the virus lead to a remedy, it ended up leading to the cure for a devastating illness ... Alzheimer's.

The cure created a super ARC protein.

The world truly rejoiced and that wasn't an understatement. Unless folks were in the latter two stages of the disease, they started to return to reality.

Clinical tests and studies were pushed through at hyper speed and before long, not only was it cured, but two years almost to the date of my cure, a vaccination was available. They said something like eighty percent of all men, women and children received it.

Not me, nor the others with ARC. They said we didn't need it.

So, it surprised me to see them talking about ARC as a virus again.

"Yeah, I did have that," I said. "Is it back?"

"Well, they're calling it ARC-2."

"ARC-2? You mean like a sequel?" I chuckled.

"You're funny. But yeah, you would think with all of us getting the vaccination we wouldn't get it."

"Maybe the vaccination for the cure only lasted so long. Who knows?"

"Yeah, but ... didn't they use the cured virus to make the Alzheimer vaccination? I mean, you would think we'd be immune."

"Maybe that's why they call it ARC-2," I said. "I don't know. I'm not a scientist. What are they saying?"

"They're aren't worried, I mean, after all they know how to beat it, but they're just expecting a lot more people to get it this time."

"Did they say why?"

Eddie shook his head. "Not really. Someone said because it's winter and things spread easier then."

"Well, I guess Velcro shoes are gonna make a comeback."

"Okay, that's not funny. I won't wear the Velcro shoes. I remember how you looked." Eddie reached for the flyer. "I'm excited to see this. My brother did the layout. He just got his degree online for graphic design."

"He did make our job easier," I replied. "We just needed to print."

At first Eddie opened it up, looking at the middle. He nodded approvingly. "Looks good." He looked at the front. "Yeah it …" His face just froze in this shocked expression.

"What? What's wrong? You got that ARC sequel virus?" I joked.

"It's wrong."

"Wrong? What do you mean, wrong? Eddie, you proofed that before we printed it."

Eddie glanced up.

"You didn't proof it?"

He exhaled loudly. "No."

"What is it? Where's the error?"

"How do you spell bologna."

"Oh, that's easy," I replied. "Even before I had super memory, I used to think of that old song my dad would sing. My bologna has a first name … and it would end with Oscar Mayer has a way with …"

Eddie handed me the flyer.

I stifled a laugh. "B-o-l-o-g-n-s?"

"None of us noticed. Do we have time to reprint?"

"Yeah, but, no reason to. No one will notice it in the store, they'll be too busy buying it. And if they do, we'll tell them it's how they spell it out in California."

"Okay, yeah, that works." Eddie took the flyer. "Other than that, they look good."

"Alright then." I set the box on the floor. "I'll leave these and probably see ya tomorrow here at the store."

"Tomorrow? Don't you mean Friday for the sale?"

"Heck no." I shook my head. "For as much as I love B-o-l-o-g-n-s. I'm gonna avoid the madhouse here. I mean after all, there is the virus again and it's winter, a crowded store, things spread."

We both had a good laugh about it. However, I stopped laughing when I stepped from his office and the words I said registered.

I joked about a virus in the winter spreading in a crowded store.

That was true, but the ARC virus, at least the one I caught, was spread by mosquitos. Last I checked, there weren't many mosquitos in the dead of winter.

<><><><>

There were times a man could bask in pride over the creation of the person he loved. Then there were times he just had to fake it.

My wife. My beautiful wife Maranda. She never aged to me and was just as breathtaking as the day I met her in the ninth grade. I swore I fell in love with her in ninth grade science when she said to me, *"Travis Grady, I am not gonna fail this assignment because you refuse to dissect our frog."*

We passed. Of course, I made her do it.

I went up to our home to check on the kids before I sought her out.

They were playing a video game. It was a 'big brother little sister' moment I loved to see.

My son was thirteen, my daughter five. Both their fingers move frantically, arms swung out as they cheered in the game. Although I knew my daughter wasn't really playing, her controller was off.

After making sure they were fine, I found Maranda.

She worked in the back of her shop, and I knew she was painting because the gallery was closed.

"What do you think?" she asked, stepped back from her

painting.

I folded my arms, tilted my head and stared at it.

"Travis?"

Usually, at least ninety percent of the time, I could figure out what she was painting. A running man, old lady eating a rose ... yep, I saw it. But for the life of me, I stared at her latest painting, not only trying to figure out what she was attempting to make with all the green paint, but if she was anywhere near finished. However, it was impossible.

"You don't like it," she said.

"No, no it's beautiful. The colors are awesome. What is it?"

"Really?" she asked with a smile. "You of all people, the king of classic television doesn't know what this is?"

"Um ...." I racked my brains. She was right, I was the king of classic television. I loved all those old shows. So much so I convinced her to let me name our son, Beau after my favorite show, Dukes of Hazzard. She had changed the spelling of the name, but was great with me calling our daughter, Daisy. I was pretty sure if we had one more son, he'd be Luke.

"Let me say it again," she said. "You, the king of classic television, can't figure this out?"

"I am not seeing how this big green painting has anything to do with ... oh!" I snapped my finger. "Hulk."

"Yes, well, more rage inspired."

"But it's not Hulk."

"No, it's rage," she said.

"Are you mad?"

She laughed. "No, I came across one of your comics today and I thought about it. But maybe I'll transform it to the Hulk or a green monster for you. Since the only television shows you watch are the classics from the seventies and eighties."

"I'll have you know, I liked Dr. Quinn Medicine Woman, too and that is neither seventies, eighties or classic."

"Yeah, I'm pretty sure Dr. Quinn Medicine Woman is classic." She started to organize.

"Speaking of Dr. Quinn."

"Well, that's an odd segue," she said.

"Not really. Did you know my virus is back? Not me, personally, but back in general?"

"Oh, yeah, I heard something about that. A lot of cases, but I'm not worried," Maranda said. "I mean, I had the shot."

"The shot is for Alzheimer's."

She shrugged. "There's a cure, Travis. It's not deadly, it never killed anyone. Just messed them up for a short spell. And besides, if I get it." She leaned into me and kissed me. "You can tie my shoes."

"Ha, ha, ha. Okay, I'm gonna start dinner."

"I'll be up in a bit."

I started to leave the back room when I noticed she was just standing there, she froze and didn't move. "Maranda? You okay?"

"Yeah ... I just don't know what I did with the blue paint I had. For the love of God, where the heck did I put it? I know I had it." She paused, then glanced to me and probably noticed me staring. "Travis, stop. I know exactly what you're thinking. You did this when you were sick. You worried every time someone forgot something that they had it. I don't have ARC, okay? I'm fine. Go make supper."

"Pasta?"

"That works."

I tapped my hand on the doorframe as I left her work area.

Hating to use Connor's word, but yeah, I guess I was being silly. I just hated having that virus. Forgetting how to tie your own shoes was ridiculously minor compared to what some of the other people had endured. Some forgot how to talk or couldn't remember who they were.

But even something so simple as the shoe thing was scary. It was like walking into a room and forgetting why you did it. That moment of confusion, only it didn't go away, ever. The confusion remained until the fog finally lifted.

For the sake of those who got the new version of ARC, I hoped for their sanity the fog lifted from their minds a lot faster than mine had.

THREE – FIRST SIGN

February 6

It snowed.

Not enough to close the schools or to cause problems on the roads, but enough to send folks flocking to Dewalt's to stock up. They all felt the need to get supplies because of the storm predicted to hit in a couple of days.

Winter panic shopping, combined with 'buy one, get one deli meat' sale, made for a madhouse. And to top it off I wasn't even supposed to be there.

I especially didn't want to be there now with everyone panic shopping.

I hated crowded stores. Even though they were my neighbors, they stopped being neighborly while they waited in line to check out.

It especially brought out my PTSD I had acquired during the ARC scare. The ARC virus I got was rare, very few people got it, yet so many worried it was going to sweep the world, it took Eddie six weeks to get back to full stock.

This time, even though it was reported about on the news quite a bit, I had stopped worrying so much about ARC-2. They still claimed it was carried by insects, so to me, I rationalized it was for the folks in Florida and California to worry about. Not us, we had snow.

Was it truly out of my mind or was it tucked away waiting to jump out and consume my every thought? I honestly didn't know.

There were like four buggies remaining outside the store

and I knew as soon as I saw that, it was going to be insane.

"Let's just come back," I told Maranda.

"Travis, no, we're here, let's get the stuff."

"But the kids will be home from school in an hour, we'll never make it back."

"I'll text Beau and tell him to watch Daisy. You just hate stores when they're like this, so stop." She marched straight into the store, leaving me to follow.

I grabbed one of the remaining carts. The handle was still wet from the snow. I pushed it inside.

Maranda stopped for one of those flyers. She knew my company printed them, and being a teacher, for sure was going to scold me about that typo.

I waited while she flipped through it.

"Well, well, well," Eddie's voice carried to me. "I thought you weren't coming in for the sale today. Hey, Maranda."

"Hey, Eddie," she looked up from the flyer. "We wouldn't miss the super sale. Love the energy in here."

"Oh, good."

"So, Eddie," Maranda said. "What is this deli meat, Bologns? The picture looks like bologna."

"Yep." Eddie nodded. "It is, but it's Californian Bologna and it's called Bologns"

"Have you tried it?" she asked Eddie. "Is it good?"

"Oh, it's real good."

"Excellent." Maranda folded the flyer. "We have to get some. Maybe a couple pounds and we'll freeze the rest."

"What?" I asked, shocked. "No one eats bologna in our house."

"Yeah, but it's California bologns, so I bet it's different."

"Heads up. The deli line is long," Eddie said.

"I bet." Maranda placed the flyer in the cart. "Travis, I'll start shopping, why don't you go get in the deli line?"

"Do I have to?"

"Yes."

"Fine. Meet you there." I looked at Eddie. "Thanks a lot." I turned around. "What all am I getting?"

"Whatever they have on the buy one, get one, and don't forget the Bologns."

Shaking my head, I just walked away. I dreaded the deli line. Knowing full well what deli sale days were like at Dewalt, I was willing to wager there was going to be at least twenty people ahead of me.

Of course, the grab and go luncheon meat section only had the items not on sale and I had to grab a number. Granted, it was annoying I had to stand in that line, but I did get a few good laughs.

Just listening to people asking for that 'Californian Bologns' was hilarious.

Heck, even the deli clerk corrected me when I asked for 'Bologna', it made for a better experience.

Albeit, a long experience for sure.

Arms full of deli meat, like eight packets of it, I found Maranda. It struck me how long I was in the deli line when I saw her ready to take on the massive checkout lanes.

If I thought the deli line was long, the checkout line screamed snowpocalypse.

At least Dewalt's was stocked up. Maranda kept smacking my hands when I reached for a magazine.

I had to remind her we weren't kids and if I wanted to read it in line I would, if I wanted to buy it, unlike when I was younger, I could.

It was just the line was moving so damn slow, and it wasn't just our line.

I watched the woman ahead of me, probably my mother's age, get her tally and swipe her card.

Then she just tilted her head and chuckled. "I can't remember my pin number."

"Really?" asked the clerk.

"Oh my goodness, it must be old age, I for the life of me can't remember it."

"It happens," the clerk said.

"Does it?" she asked, concern in her voice.

I spoke up, "I can never remember the pin when I take my wife's card. You know what? Swipe it as credit."

"Can I?" the lady asked.

"Yeah, just … uh …" I made my way to her. "Hit that little red X there."

"Won't it cancel?"

"No, watch."

On the display it popped up 'bypass pin and run as credit'

"Oh, look at that," the woman said. "Now, I really feel dumb."

"Happens to us all," I told her. "We all for …" I cleared my throat. "Forget things."

Maranda grumbled my name. "Travis."

She knew me as well as I knew myself, and she knew where my mind immediately went. She warned me a couple more times before we even got to our car. A glance to the man looking for his truck, another at a woman who searched frantically in her purse.

I thought about the woman in the deli line who took five minutes because she couldn't think of what she wanted, finally telling the clerk to give her whatever was on sale.

Maybe it was my paranoia over the ARC virus, even though I knew there was a cure, something about this new wave bothered me.

FOUR – OVER COOKED

February 12

The virus story had hit the ten day point. I always considered it a tipping point when it came to news stories, by ten days the story went away or got bigger. Along the lines of, did it use up its fifteen minutes of fame, or did it glorify and explode?

The story on ARC-2 grew bigger, but it was baffling as well.

Everything they thought they knew about it was tossed out the window the moment the first northern state confirmed a case.

It still wasn't wide spread nor labeled a pandemic. Most people didn't fear it at all because not only had they been through round one three years earlier, they knew it wasn't fatal.

No one died from it.

It was easy for people to say the virus was nothing when it didn't affect them or they themselves hadn't caught it.

For me it was absolutely terrifying to have, to not know something you should. To wake up every morning wondering what you had forgotten, and if you did, was it something important or someone you loved?

I read my news online like most people. Every morning I checked to see if it was there, if so, was it a top story or did it make its way down the line.

I didn't want to read about it, I just wanted to see it was beaten. For the first several days every story was optimistic, then they kind of disappeared. Older stories from days earlier would make their way into the feed, just to fill the gaps.

Had I not known better, I would have thought it was over or fading, but I did know better. The stats and information were there, a person just needed to know where to look.

The Centers for Disease Control and World Health Organization all carried the information.

I had my morning routine. News, then those sites.

"You are gonna drive yourself nuts," Maranda said, setting an empty plate before me that morning.

"I am just ..." I noticed the plate. "What?" I laughed. "Is this your subtle hint to make me go on a diet?"

"What?" she asked confused.

I didn't say anything, I just shifted my eyes from her to the plate a few times. Finally, she looked down.

"Oh, gees, sorry." She grabbed the plate and walked to the stove. "And don't give me that look. I was too busy planning on scolding you."

"That you forgot to put food on my plate?" I asked.

"She could be telling you something," my son spoke up. "Maybe she's saying, get your own food."

"Mommy's funny," Daisy giggled.

"There was no hidden message." Maranda put my pancakes before me. "I was just preoccupied." She slipped into the chair next to me.

"Yeah," I said. "You making breakfast like this is just like one of my old television shows."

"Travis," Maranda laughed. "What are you talking about?"

"You making breakfast," I said. "You never make breakfast."

"Yes, I do."

"No ... you don't."

"Travis, I do. I make breakfast all the time." She reached for the syrup. "I made French toast yesterday."

"Maybe when I wasn't here."

"You ate four pieces."

"Are you joking me?" I asked. "Cause it's not funny."

"I'm not joking and this isn't a joke. I make breakfast. Ask the kids."

"Maranda, I think we should know. Wait." I paused. "Do you make breakfast? Maybe you do and I just forgot. God damn virus on the brain. No pun intended."

"Travis, you're scaring me," she said. "Stop. Okay. It's not funny."

I mumbled. "No, it's not."

"And oh, shoot?" she lifted her phone. "I have to call Tracy to see if she can come in to the gallery today. I have to deliver a painting." She stood with her phone and walked off.

I exhaled, whistling softly and grabbed the syrup. "I'm losing it. It's like the shoe thing all over. Honestly, guys it's like I can't remember the last time she made breakfast."

"Dad," Beau said my name.

"Yeah?"

He looked over his shoulder, then back to me as he leaned forward and dropped his voice to a whisper. "It's not the shoe thing again."

"What do you mean?"

"You're not forgetting anything. You can't remember the last time she made breakfast because she never ..." Beau said. "She never does. Ever."

I was worried when I thought it was *my* memory that was going, until Beau commented, then suddenly I found myself dismissing it and finding reasons for my wife's strange behavior. Because realistically, what were the odds the rare virus would make its way back into our home again?

Honestly, I maybe could have found reasons for Maranda's absentmindedness, but unfortunately, every reason circled back to ARC-2.

Her comment about going into the shop was the catalyst for making me even more concerned.

Everyone was talking about how there were three suspected cases in our town and two over in West Raven, near the Walmart.

"Five in this small area?" I asked, fiddling with my coffee cup in the break room. "How do you know?"

Conner replied, "I saw Chief Fisher at the café. He was telling me, all three were admitted to the hospital last night, two for loss of memory and the other for a violent outburst, but they couldn't speak to the reason."

"Are you shitting me? Do we know about the ones in West Raven?"

Connor shook his head. "Chief only knew details of ours. Three incidents, three different times, people that don't even know each other."

I whistled. "That's kind of scary, did they confirm?"

"I don't know that either. I mean, how do they test?"

"Spinal tap," I answered. "That's how they tested me. But ... how is that even possible? The virus had been eradicated. It's bloodborne. Its main route of transmission is insects, it's the dead of winter."

"Spiders," Connor said assuredly. "Spiders, bed bugs, lice ... they're all insects. That's just my guess. People hear insects they don't think of those, or cockroaches."

"Yeah, I guess."

"While you're guessing, can you guess what I'm gonna ask? Can you run the ads down to Furniture Outlet?"

"Sure, I want to stop at Reilly's for wings."

"Grab me an order?" Connor asked.

"Yep. I might stop down and talk to the chief."

"Why?" Connor questioned.

"More info," I said, not wanting to tell him about Maranda.

"I'm sure he knows very little, but you can try. "I know you're worried. It was scary when you had it. But there is one good thing." He finished his coffee, crushed the paper cup and tossed it in the trash. "It's not deadly."

The lack of lethality was a good thing, the only good thing about the ARC virus.

<><><><>

If we hadn't lived in such a small town, I was certain the chief would have told me he was too busy to discuss it, even if he was just playing on his phone.

I had stopped in to see him after the furniture warehouse drop off.

The chief was in.

He was a no nonsense kind of guy, with an attitude from an era gone by. Not too big, average looking guy in his early sixties. Several times he was lambasted for being politically incorrect.

That was just who he was.

"Travis, I think you're worrying about this too much," he said, sitting across from me.

"I wouldn't say worrying about it. Curious is more like it."

"I say something to your boss and here you are."

"Yeah, but I mean, three people?"

"Two weeks ago, we had nine people with the flu. Five went to the hospital, I didn't see you here."

"This is different," I said. "It really is."

"You think maybe you feel different about it because you had such a hard time when you had it? I mean, we all felt bad about the Velcro shoes."

"It was more than Velcro shoes, it was that a part of my brain went blank," I replied.

"Is it still blank?" he asked.

"Well, no."

"And the brains of the ones who went to the hospital won't be blank for long either. They haven't even been confirmed to have it."

"How do you know?" I asked.

"I called. I followed up. If this thing is breaking out here, I want to know, but the doctors at the hospital didn't seem too concerned, neither should we."

"Maybe you're right. Maybe this has to do with me having it."

"Bet it does. If you want to feel better, why don't you call the doctor that worked with you on it? The big virus guy, bet he could put your mind at ease."

"Which one?" I asked. "I mean I could call any of them."

"The one that coined the phrase the Great Eight."

The Great Eight. There was a term I hadn't heard in a couple years. That was what they referred to us as, the eight people whose consistent tests results showed the super evolved ARC protein that led to the cure.

"Oh yeah, him, he was an epidemiologist." I nodded. "I might reach out."

"Let me know what he says, if you don't mind."

"I will and thank you." I stood.

"And Travis, honestly, I don't think there's anything to worry about. It could be anything."

"You're right, and all I'm gonna worry about is getting my wings."

"You headed down to Reilly's?" Chief asked.

"Yep. It's fifty cent whole wings night."

"Can you grab me an order?"

"Sure thing."

I thanked him once more and apologized for bothering him and left the station. When I got in my truck, I pulled out my phone and called home.

"Hey, hon," Maranda answered the phone. "Everything okay?"

"It is. Why do you ask?"

"You don't usually call during the day."

That made me smile, because I didn't. "You're right," I told her. "Two reasons. I'm headed to Reilly's for wings, did you want some?"

"No, I'm headed out. But thank you."

"That is the second reason," I said. "You told me you have a painting to deliver, you didn't mention where and I didn't know if you need me home for the kids."

"Oh, I should be back. It's not even one yet. I'm only going to West Raven to drop it off to Mary Wells."

"Mary Wells, why does that name sound familiar?" I asked.

"Probably because she lived here in town and just moved. I mentioned she commissioned me to do that painting of her mother for her new house."

"Yeah, probably, weird because I remember everything."

"Not everything, Travis," Maranda stated. "Just what you decide to embed to memory."

"True. So, you'll be home?"

"Unless her and I get to talking."

"Which is possible," I said. "I'll get home early anyhow, so Beau isn't stuck babysitting for long."

"Sounds good," she said. "Enjoy those wings."

"I will and be safe. There's a little snow on the ground."

"Oh, it's just a bit. I'm not worried. The tires are good."

"Just be safe."

"I will," she replied.

We exchanged our 'end of the call I love you' and I hung up.

After talking to Maranda, I felt better. She sounded fine and, for the time being, I was more concerned about getting my wings.

<><><><>

Reilly's was located east, a mile out of town. It was more of a neighborhood bar than restaurant. After a certain time of night, the food stopped cooking and the booze flowed. They had music three nights a week.

It wasn't a great big place, about the size of a diner, and it attracted a lot of customers from the highway. Probably because of that tall, obnoxious neon sign with a horseshoe, like it was some Irish place.

I was surprised when I pulled up and only saw two cars in the lot. It was lunch time on wing special day, it should have been jumping. Then again, there was a glaze of snow on the ground and people always got scared when it snowed.

At least I wouldn't feel like a pain in the butt when I went in during lunch rush to get four orders of Reilly's special sauce wings.

I had to get an order for Beau.

When I stepped in, I didn't see anyone. I could smell food cooking and the television behind the bar was playing along with the jukebox.

I walked to the bar and there was a drink sitting there, so someone was around. I grabbed my phone, shooting Connor a text to let him know I thought Reilly's was short staffed and it would be a little bit. Just as I hit send and set my phone on the bar, I glanced up to the news.

I couldn't really make out what the woman was saying with the music playing, but I was stunned when I saw the words, seventeen thousand confirmed.

The squeak then slam of the door caught my attention, I thought maybe it was George the bartender, but it was some guy about my age coming out of the bathroom. I could tell right away he was a traveler. A fancy one. He had perfect dark hair, he wore what looked like designer jeans and a dressy button down shirt.

Totally out of place for our town.

Returning my attention to the television, I must have muttered out loud when I thought, "Seventeen thousand? Would that be cases?"

"It would be," the man from the bathroom stood next to me and grabbed the drink. "Seventeen thousand cases, more each day."

"Of ARC?" I asked.

"Yep." He sipped his drink.

I whistled. "Holy cow."

"I'll tell you though." He lifted his drink using it to point to the television. "That won't be me." He took a sip.

"How do you know? Did you have it?"

"No, I didn't get the vaccination."

"I'm sorry?" I asked confused.

"The Alzheimer's vaccine, I didn't get it."

"You think that's what's causing this?"

"Without a doubt, then again, I don't believe in scientific medication or rather, western medicine. No, let me rephrase, I prefer Eastern Medicine. Sometimes there's a place for Western medicine."

"Eastern, Western," I said. "You mean like New York Versus California?"

He chuckled and took another sip, set down his drink, reached for his wallet. "No, I mean, traditional Chinese medicine. That's called Eastern." He pulled out a card and handed it to me.

"Doctor Jon Yee," I read it. "Are you a real doctor?"

"I am. I went to UCLA."

"Oh, your card says your office is in Nevada, you're a long way from home. You driving?"

"I am. I had a conference in Atlanta. I hate flying. I'd rather drive. I always do," Jon said. "It's my first time through here. It's nice. Snowy, but nice."

"Just be careful, they don't get to the roads right away." I extended the card back to him.

"Keep it. You may be out my way sometime."

"Doubt it, but who knows." I stuck the card in my pocket. "I will say, you picked a good place to get food. Reilly's has the best wings. Did you get Reilly's special sauce?"

"I did. So, they'll be worth the wait?"

"Absolutely," I replied.

"They do take a while."

"How long have you been waiting?"

He looked down at his watch. "Over twenty minutes. He's been back there a while. I think he burned the first batch though."

I sniffed. Jon was right, something was burning. It wasn't hardcore burning, but a hint of 'over done' filled the air. "And you said George has been back there this whole time?"

"I guess. I don't know if that's his name or not."

"Weird." I inched down the bar nearer to the kitchen door. "Hey, George!" I hollered out. "George, it's Travis."

"So, this is unusual for him to stay back there?" Jon asked.

"Yeah, it is."

"You think he's alright?"

"I'll find out."

"I'll come with you." After one more drink, nearly finishing his glass, Jon set it down and walked toward me.

As soon as I opened the kitchen door, I saw the smoke. It wasn't thick and black, more like gray and it carried a strange smell.

"Hey, George, *whatcha* do?" I called out. "Burn the wings?" It wasn't so thick that I wouldn't see him.

Jon did. He saw George before I did.

Blurting out a shocked, "Jesus," Jon brushed by me and raced forward. That was when I saw George.

He stood next to the two basket deep fryers. No expression on his face, eyes forward in a lost stare while his arm, up to the elbow, was submerged in the frying oil.

Steam poured up and he didn't react, not to the burning, the pain or our presence.

Jon reached him, looked at me and ordered, "Call 911." He braced George and reached for his arm.

I nodded quickly, stumbling back, reaching for my phone.

I had left it on the bar.

"Now." Jon lifted George's arm from the grease and the flesh bubbled and just oozed off his bones, dripping into the hot oil and sizzling.

It was traumatic, I wanted to vomit, but I didn't. I hurried out of the kitchen, swiping up my phone without stopping, and I called for help.

FIVE – MARY WELLS

Can't talk. My text to Connor read.

Just tell me what happened.

I can't. It's bad. I may go home. But I'll stop by and tell you. Or call.

You're not making sense, Connor replied.

Nothing is.

It didn't take long for help to arrive. But it seemed like forever. Of course, George had help. Jon was a doctor. I'm glad he was there, I wouldn't have known what to do if it was just me.

When I returned from the call, Jon had George on the floor, his head resting on Jon's legs as he covered the arm with an apron.

"They're on their way," I said. "Is that his apron?"

"Yeah."

"Want me to find one that's clean."

"It's not gonna matter," Jon spoke soft.

I expect some sort of reaction out of George, but there was nothing. He just stared. "Is he?"

Jon shook his head. "No. I don't even think he's in shock."

"Can I do anything?"

"Go wait for help."

That was good enough for me and I left the kitchen again. I heard the sirens as soon as I stepped into the dining room. Chief Fisher raced into Reilly's.

"What's going on?" he asked me. "What happened? The call was a severe burn."

"It's worse than severe, Chief, if that's possible. It's George. He's in the kitchen."

Chief Fisher didn't wait for me to even explain what happened, he ran to the kitchen. Less than a minute later, the firefighters came in, then the paramedics.

I didn't want to be in the way, so I sat at the bar. That's when I sent a text to Connor and Maranda. Both messages said the same thing, *'Something bad happened at Reilly's, hit me back when you can'*, Connor got back to me right away.

I wanted a drink, I wanted one badly. I even thought about going behind the bar for one. My hands shook out of control, my heart raced, it was singularly the worst thing I had seen in my life.

It had to be a good fifteen minutes and I couldn't figure out what was happening. Didn't they want to get him to the hospital? Or life flight him to Knoxville?

Finally, looking as if he too had been traumatized, Chief Fisher came from the back. Behind him was Jon.

Chief shook his head and walked behind the bar. "He's gone."

"Oh my God." I dropped to a bar stool.

The Chief grabbed a couple glasses and set them on the bar. "Doc?"

"Please."

"Travis."

"Um ... yeah, please."

"They're gonna take him to the hospital, even though he's gone. Fire crew is cleaning up." Chief Fisher poured a shot worth in each glass. "I talked to his sister."

"Not his wife?" I asked.

"No, um, Sadie is on shift at the hospital, his sister is going to go over and tell her. I just thought it would be better coming from family and not on the phone." He slid the glasses our way. "Thank you for your help, Doc."

"Not a problem. I'm sorry, I couldn't do more," Jon said.

"Would that Eastern medicine have helped?" I asked.

"Nothing. I don't even know how he was still standing. He pretty much lost most of his blood," Jon replied.

"What happened?" I asked.

Chief answered. "Fire crew thinks he slipped. He tried to catch himself and went into the grease."

Jon hurried and finished his drink, setting down the glass when they paramedics came out with George's covered body. "I'm going to go with them. So I can be there if his wife has any questions."

"We appreciate that Doc," Chief said. "You don't have to."

"I know. I want to." He gave a pat to my back "Travis, call me if you need to talk. You have my number. Or just text me, if you want. Okay?"

"Yeah, thank you."

He was a nice guy, genuine. He didn't need to jump into action, but he did. I could tell by the Chief's face he was waiting for everyone to leave. When they did, he poured more in my glass.

"I'm driving," I said.

"Yes, well, that won't raise your blood alcohol, not at your weight. And I won't pull you over."

"Thanks. I need this and I am not a big drinker."

"I don't think anything is making that go away." Chief sipped his drink. "Travis." He set down his glass. "I need you to get in touch with that doctor or epidemiologist you know. I really want to talk to him and get some answers."

"Answers to?" I asked. "Chief, you don't think ..."

"I don't know, Travis. I don't know if this was ARC, but I do know this," Chief said. "George didn't fall into that grease."

<><><><>

Maranda was always telling me my super memory was conditioned on things I wanted to remember. Like a phone number or a birthdate, or when the testing site gave me a list and four hours later I could recite it in order.

The image of George's arm would be embedded in my brain for the rest of my life. No matter how much I didn't want to recall it.

On the positive side, I remembered the epidemiologist well. He and I had talked a lot. I also remembered the number to his lab. His last name was Collins, but I just called him Richard. He was a nice guy, a family man who said everything he did, he did for the future of his kids and grandkids.

Before I even left the parking lot of Reilly's, I called him. He didn't answer, I got his voicemail and left a message. I was certain he would call me back.

There was a look of deep concern on Chief Fisher's face that I hadn't seen. It made me wonder if there were more people he knew about but just wasn't saying.

It was still early. I tried to call Maranda and she didn't answer. The roads were starting to get bad so I left her a message to be careful. I didn't want to say anymore, she probably was having fun with her friend about her painting and I didn't want to ruin that.

My appetite had completely left, but I knew I had to occupy my mind. I went back to the shop to drop off the invoice from Furniture Warehouse. I could have just held on to it, but a part of me wanted to talk about what I saw, what worried me.

Connor was a friend.

"Jesus, Travis, I'm sorry you had to see that."

"It was pretty bad."

"What happened?" Connor asked. "If he didn't fall into the fryer. How the hell else did that happen?"

"I think Chief thinks it was the ARC."

"ARC? Travis, I don't recall ever hearing stories like this with the first round. Did you?"

I shook my head. "No, it was memory, but what if he just forgot what he was doing? I mean, that's possible, and then again, what if we just never heard the horror stories."

"His poor wife and kids."

"I know ... Connor, I saw on the news there's like close to twenty thousand people with it."

"How is that possible? There was the vaccine."

"Maybe they never got it," I said. "I mean I remember Richard, that doctor, telling me twenty-percent of all people who could get it, didn't."

"So the ARC makes a comeback and now they aren't immune like the rest of us."

"Exactly. The guy at Reilly's, he was a doctor, he said the vaccine caused this."

"Oh, nonsense." Connor waved out his hand. "You know as well as I do, that's not the case. These are people who didn't get vaccinated."

"I hope you're right. Well, I'm gonna head on home, maybe stop at the store. I'll cook dinner for Maranda and the kids."

"They'll like that," Connor said. "Travis, keep me posted if you hear anything."

"I will."

I wanted to hear something, I was hoping my phone would ring. I kept checking it, wondering if it was even working.

My mind kept going to George and the fact that if he did have ARC, the prospect of it was scary. I forgot how to tie my shoes and forgot what I had for lunch, I couldn't fathom going into a state that put me or others into danger.

I accepted ARC cases on name value, I had to look into it more. It made me rethink things. Look at things differently. In the store I watched people I passed, were they behaving strangely? Did they look lost? Then again, people were rushing because the roads were getting covered in snow.

A part of me couldn't wait to get home and get on my computer. The words were larger and not as slow as my phone.

I picked up stuff to make barbecue chicken, the kids always liked that, Maranda, too.

The Gallery was dark and I didn't see Maranda's car, so I knew she wasn't back yet.

Balancing the grocery bags, I made my way up to our home. I had time to get things put away and make a snack for the kids.

Man, I needed to see my kids.

I put the bags down, then put away what I wasn't using right away and checked out the time on my phone, then checked to see if I had a missed call from my wife. It wasn't like her not to reply. I hated to be a helicopter husband, but I did need to talk to her.

Just as I was about to call her, my phone rang. A number I didn't recognize.

"Hello," I answered.

"Travis?" the woman said.

"Yeah."

"Hey, this is Sadie Reilly."

"Oh my gosh, Sadie, I am so sorry. I am. George was a great guy."

"Thank you, Travis. They said you were with him."

I cringed.

"I knew something was gonna happen," she said. "I knew it. I had this weird feeling. He was acting so absent-minded this morning."

"Just today?" I asked.

"He was so scattered brained, I just had a bad feeling. You were there, Travis. Did he suffer? Did he call out for us?" she asked. "I need to know his last words."

"Sadie, he was in a state of shock when we found him. I ... I'm not a doctor, but I don't think he was suffering. But ... hold on." I reached into my back pocket and pulled out the business card "There was a guy there, he actually is a doctor. He went to the hospital with Travis."

"Oh, Doctor Yee?"

"Yes. You met him?"

"I did. But he didn't know George like you did, so he was not able to say if George acted different."

"Did he tell you George didn't suffer."

"He said that he felt strongly that George wasn't in pain," Sadie said. "I just, you know, again, wanted to hear from you because you knew him. And thank you for being there."

"You're welcome, and if you need anything, don't hesitate to call."

She thanked me. I could only imagine what she was going

through. For some reason, I put that card on the fridge under a magnet, not that I would use it again, and I hurriedly started supper and got the popcorn going so the kids had something to munch on.

I didn't tell them what happened, just I had some work to do on the computer. After getting them set up with their homework at the kitchen table, I went to the computer in the living room.

The moment I started looking up ARC-2, I went down the rabbit hole. I took notes on things I read; strange stories people shared on social media. I watched video after video.

Everyone was an expert and no one knew anything.

They argued how it spread and if the people that got it, had been inoculated.

It was strange because there was so much information, yet, everything was vague. The first record case of ARC-2 was in Brussels two months earlier.

"Dad?" Beau called my name, snapping me out of my research world.

"Yep? What's up?"

"Your timer went off."

"Oh, it did?" I turned in the chair and stood. "Thanks. I was all wrapped up. That went by ..." I completely froze. "So fast."

"Dad?"

I reached back and grabbed the phone. I had been so busy, I totally didn't think about the fact that I hadn't heard from Maranda.

"Where's your sister?" I asked.

"In her room."

"Thanks." I hurried into the kitchen, took the pan out of the oven and shut off the stove. "I'll be right back."

"Where are you going?" Beau asked.

"Down to the gallery, bet your mother just went right to work. She was working on that green painting. I want... I want to get her for dinner."

"Okay. You think she's back from West Raven?"

"Yeah, she has to be. Set the table," I instructed, then made it to the back hall. There was a stairwell there that went right down to the gallery.

I knew a part of me was lying not only to Beau but to myself about Maranda being in the gallery.

As soon as I made it to the bottom, opened the door and saw it was dark. My fears were confirmed. Maranda hadn't made it back.

I flipped the lights on in the gallery, then called as I made my way to the door.

Her phone went right to voice mail.

A sickening feeling hit my gut, worsened when I saw it was dark and the snow falling hard.

I wanted to leave, go look for her, and I would but first I called the Chief. I knew he had patrols, they could help look for her.

"Loudon, Police Department. This is Chief Fisher speaking," he answered.

"Hey Chief, it's Travis Grady."

"Hey, Travis, you hear from that scientist friend of yours?"

"No, sir, but I have a problem," I said.

"What is it?"

"My wife went to West Raven to drop off a painting this afternoon, she hasn't come back. I called, but no answer. Now her phone is going straight to voicemail. I'm worried, it looks bad out there."

"What time was this?"

"A little before one," I replied. "I know, I sound like a horrible husband not calling sooner."

"Oh, no. It's only five-thirty. West Raven has this place called the Rogue. My wife goes there, maybe Maranda met friends for drinks."

"Well, she was meeting a friend from here to drop off a painting. I mean she just moved there so, Maranda may be catching up."

"There you go," Chief Fisher said. "I wouldn't be worried.

Who was it?"

"Mary Wells."

Silence.

"She said Mary commissioned her to do a painting of her mother, and Maranda went to drop it off at her new house. In fact ..."

"Travis."

I turned around. "I see a blank spot. That must have been the painting."

"Travis ..."

"I thought that painting was here a long time. Guess I was wrong."

"It was," Chief Fisher said.

"I'm sorry?"

"Travis, did Maranda tell you this?"

"Yes," I answered. "I knew the name sounded familiar. It's not like me to forget things, but I guess ..."

"Travis, Mary Wells died four years ago. The day she moved from town she was killed in that accident on Seventy-Five."

"Oh my God, I remember that. I remember Maranda hanging that painting after she died. It didn't register."

"No, because it was four years ago," Chief Fisher said.

Was it me? Immediately, I panicked. What if I wasn't remembering? What if Maranda told me something totally different? I rushed to the appointment book at the desk in the gallery.

"Travis, you there? You want me to start looking and get in touch with West Raven?"

I flipped open the book, and sure enough written under today's date, in Maranda's handwriting was, 'Mary Wells, One-Thirty.'.

I got sick, immediately sick. "Yeah, Chief, please," I said. "Help me find my wife."

SIX – INSIGHTS

One of the hardest things I had to do was pretend everything was alright, when I knew it wasn't. Putting on a front for my kids was nothing but lying. As the unexpected snow fell harder and faster, it increasingly became more difficult to hide my concern.

My wife had not returned, and I couldn't help but think her missing had much to do with her memory lapses that had started earlier in the day.

Maybe they started before that and I just didn't notice.

Visions of George and his arm extended into that vat of hot grease played over in my mind. I couldn't shake the worst case scenarios that I envisioned about wife.

I served my children dinner, while watching my phone for any messages or texts. Finally, after the dishes were tossed in the sink and I got Daisy settled some, I told Beau what was going on.

Chief Fisher, two squad cars and a West Raven officer were out there looking. It was three hours since I called the chief and still nothing.

I relented.

Knowing no one would make it out in the weather, I asked Chief Fisher to help me find someone to sit with the kids while I went out and helped in the search.

He didn't think I needed to, but understood. The Chief's own sister came to my home to be there, while I went out.

I told Beau I would call him and let him know what was going on.

Then I drove.

No radio, I had to focus, look around.

The snow blocked out the sounds of the world, adding a hypnotic quiet to the night. The only sounds were my tires crunching against the snow and the blade swiping the thick flakes from my windshield.

My destination wasn't West Raven, it was east.

We all assumed that was where she went, but if Maranda had lost touch with reality, then surely she lost touch with her sense of direction.

I drove on the secondary route, despite it not having been cleared or treated by crews. It was the most direct way out Loudon and to the next town.

I made it there and back, not seeing anything or even a car on the road. Not even a mile away from Loudon, my phone rang, causing me to jump from my skin.

I was focused on driving, so I didn't look at who was calling, I just answered.

"Hello."

"Travis, this is Chief Fisher."

Something about his voice scared me. "Tell me she's alive."

"She ... she is," he replied. "Travis, where are you at now?"

"Almost back in town. I just passed Reilly's."

"Good. I need you to come to Weatherby's. You'll be here before the ambulance."

"Ambulance ..."

"She's fine, Travis. It's just ... it's too hard to explain."

"I'll be there in a minute." I hung up knowing it wouldn't take long to get there. Weatherby's was one of those mega pharmacy stores. It was a few blocks away, a standalone building with a large parking lot. What was she doing there? Did she think the store was open? There were a ton of questions that would be answered shortly.

The store was dark when I pulled up, just the standard exterior spotlights above the door. I could see the flashing red and blue lights coming from behind the building. The lights of the police were reflecting off the glaze of snow.

I pulled around to the back, sure enough Maranda's car was there, it was completely snow covered with the exception of a spot cleared on the windshield. The clearing of snow looked as if it were done by a hand. Two squad cars were also there. Angie, one of our officers in town stood by Maranda's car and Chief Fisher walked to me as I stopped my truck.

Leaving it running, I got out. "What's going on?"

"Angie spotted the car, I don't know how. It's not running, she won't start it. She won't get out," Chief Fisher said. "We've asked."

"I don't ... I don't understand."

"Talk to her. The ambulance will be here in a minute."

I nodded and made my way to the car.

"Hey, Maranda," Officer Angie said when I made my approach. "Look who's here."

I said a soft, "Thank you," to the officer and moved closer to the open car window.

If she was fine, I didn't understand why the ambulance had to be called until I saw her in the car.

She was pasty white and her lips were blue and her eyes had this glassy look to them.

Angie cleared her throat. "She's clearly hypothermic. She stopped shivering. She won't let me touch her to check her vitals."

"Maranda," I said, speaking directly into the window as I reached for the car handle. "Hey, sweetie. Want to open the door?"

"Don't' be silly, Travis, there's no need. Can you tell the police officers I am fine? I'm not doing anything illegal," Maranda replied.

"Maranda, it's awfully cold. At least start the car."

"No."

"Maranda, what's going on?"

"Oh my God," she said agitated. "I am back here because I am waiting until I see Brandy Thomas pull out."

"What?"

"I stopped for cigarette's Travis. Okay? I didn't want you to know and if she saw me, I am sure she would have told you. So I'm just waiting for her to leave the store, get my smokes, and then deliver this painting to Mary."

"I get that," Travis said. "And Brandy can be a big mouth. But it's awfully ..."

"Why is there an ambulance here?" she asked, looking at Angie. "Officer is someone hurt?"

"Maranda," I spoke calmly. "It's here for you. You've been out here a long time in the cold."

"Oh, nonsense, just a few ...." Her eyes shifted. "Is it dark out? How can it be dark?"

"Unlock the door, Maranda," I told her.

"Travis, what is going on?" she asked.

"Unlock it, please."

"No, I don't understand."

I didn't wait any longer, the open space of the window was wide enough for me to place my arm through. I did and reached down for the lock. I felt her hand fighting my searching fingers as she screamed at me to stop.

Then just as I touched the lock buttons, the window wound up. I hit the lock as the edge of the window jammed below my armpit. Hearing the shift of the lock and before she could lock it again, I grabbed the handle with my free hand and opened the door.

Angie raced forward, grabbing for her.

Door alarm dinging from the keys in the ignition, Maranda screamed when Angie and one of the paramedics reached for her.

She was out of control, as if strangers were abducting her. I couldn't move or help, I had to just stand by, arm trapped in the window, until they were clear enough with her for me to reach around and lower the window.

I didn't understand why she was so out of control. Not only screaming my name, but adding that she hated me.

Without a doubt it was a breakdown of sorts.

It took the Chief, Angie and both paramedics to get her into one of those ambulance stretcher chairs and strap her in.

She didn't stop fighting nor screaming even as they loaded her in the ambulance.

The EMT told me they were taking her to Loudon Medical, our small local hospital.

Loudon Medical was good for injuries and minor things, but I wasn't sure it was the right place to take Maranda.

I thanked the Chief and Angie, then followed the ambulance.

At the very least we had found her and Maranda was safe.

<><><><>

As I suspected, Loudon Medical wasn't the place for her and the attending physician told me that right away. Yet, I wasn't able to see her or talk to her, they wanted one more evaluation and then they were going to move her.

They had given her a mild sedative and asked if I could wait to sign some papers for the transfer.

I assumed it was Knoxville, and needed to make arrangements for the kids. As much as I loved my wife, I couldn't leave the kids at home with the Chief's sister, so I called my own mom, woke her up and tried my best to explain what was going on. She lived in Sweetwater, it wasn't that far and I made plans to get the kids to her the next day.

That was the plan.

I had already been at the hospital for two hours, I needed to get to my kids.

Chief Fisher stopped in to see me before he went home for the night, I told him I was very grateful and told I'd relieve his sister as soon as I was done.

While we finished our conversation, the attending ER doctor along with some woman, called for me and brought me into a back office.

The ER doctor introduced the woman, Barbara, as a nurse practitioner, from Mobile Crisis. It didn't register what that meant, because I was stuck on the word 'crisis'.

"Mr. Grady," Barbara said. "Your wife is coming out of sedation. I had a chance to speak to her briefly, but going by what Doctor Walters has told me, could you answer some questions for me?"

"Sure."

"Do you have any knowledge of your wife using a controlled substance, or having a drug problem?"

"No." I shook my head. "I told the doctor here the same thing. She has a few drinks. But doesn't do drugs. I am certain if you run a drug test you'll see that."

"Has she exhibited any odd behavior lately?" Barbara asked.

"Well, other than claiming she makes breakfast every day, delivering a painting to a dead woman, then sitting in a parking lot for ten hours, no."

Barbara looked at Doctor Walters. "Mr. Grady, we want to transport your wife to Peninsula Hospital. My job with Mobile Crisis ..."

That's when it hit me. "Wait. A psychiatric hospital?" I asked.

Barbara nodded. "Yes."

"My wife doesn't need a psychiatric hospital."

"Mr. Grady, she does," Barbara replied. "We are certain she is having a crisis and needs further evaluation."

"Yeah, medical," I said.

"Peninsula is capable of running all necessary medical testing to rule out ..."

"Can you test for ARC-2?" I asked.

Doctor Walters spoke up. "ARC-2? You think your wife has ARC 2?"

"I do. I feel it," I said.

"Even though I highly doubt she has ARC-2, they can do testing at Peninsula," Doctor Walters said.

"And treat her?" I asked. "Because if she has it, she needs

treatment."

"Mr. Grady," Barbara spoke up. "ARC is very rare, and even if she has it, we could treat it, but ... knowing ARC and what it does, how if effects the ability for individuals to operate normally ... seeing your wife's behavior, Peninsula is the best place for your wife until this crisis is over."

I didn't want to knock Peninsula. I knew it was a great place, they helped my cousin Bob. And hating to admit it, seeing how Maranda was acting, a part of me knew Peninsula would be a safe place for her. The difference between Peninsula and a regular medical center was, once I kissed my wife goodbye, it would be days until I was allowed to visit her.

It was for the best, and I knew whether it was a mental breakdown or ARC, Maranda would get the help she needed.

SEVEN - DISCHARGE

February 15

They said she didn't know. Valentine's Day had come and gone, I wasn't able to visit, and she didn't know.

It broke my heart, but it wasn't like her memory was blank. She just lived in the past a lot. The nurses updated me on her condition, or reality break as someone called it.

She was like a light switch with it, off and on. One moment sad that she wasn't with her family, fully aware that she wasn't home, then the next moment she was lost and clueless.

Innocent, like a child.

The day after Valentine's Day they called and said her seventy-two hours was up and we could come and visit. I truly wasn't sure if I wanted to bring Daisy, five years old and seeing her mother in a place like that. But one of the nurses there thought it would be a good idea and that Maranda looked lovely.

The kids were excited. Well, Daisy was. Beau was about as excited as a thirteen year old boy could get. I put Daisy in a cute little dress, made Beau comb his hair. We had flowers, we made cards, and I even wore a nice pull over shirt. Which I only wore when we occasionally went to church.

"Make sure you eat," I told Daisy. "I'm not stopping."

"Dad," Beau laughed. "You act like this is a long road trip."

"To a five year old it is," I replied. "Takes about forty-five minutes so Daisy, pee after you eat, I'm not stopping."

"I can't wait to see Mommy."

"Me, too."

"Does she miss us?" Daisy asked.

"Very much," I said. "She misses you so much and can't wait to come home."

"When can she?"

"I don't know sweetie." I grabbed her hand. "Eat."

"Hey, Dad, are they saying anything new?" Beau asked.

"Nothing. Nothing at all. But, no new news is good news, right?" My phone rang and I turned my head to where it sat on the kitchen counter. "Finish up, we're leaving in fifteen." I stood and grabbed the phone.

I knew the number as soon as I saw it.

Richard.

I hurriedly informed Beau to keep an eye on Daisy and get her ready as I grabbed my phone. "Richard," I answered. "Thank you so much for calling."

"Travis, I got all your messages."

I didn't know what to make of his tone, was he angry, tired? He didn't sound himself, then again, when I talked to him the time before he was euphoric over this cure for Alzheimer's.

"I'm sorry about that Richard, at first I called because I was hearing about ARC-2. Then it was my wife and all."

"I'm sorry for that. And I apologize for not calling you back. I did however reach out to Peninsula. They are aware who I am and they forwarded me your wife's scans so I could look."

"Wow, that is amazing, thank you so much. What about the spinal tap?" I asked. "Did they send you the results of that?"

"They didn't take spinal fluid."

"They must really not think it's ARC-2."

"Travis … she has what you have been asking about. But … there, there is no ARC-2. Or a virus, anyhow."

"Wait. What?" I asked in shock. "Yeah, there is, it's all over the news."

"One of the reasons it has taken so long to get back to you was because I really debated on whether I would tell you the truth or not. But I don't see you running to social media or the news."

"That's not me," I said.

"I know."

"What's going on Richard?" I asked. "I saw on the news the other day something like seventeen thousand people are sick. How can say seventeen thousand people have a virus when they don't."

"At first they believed it was ARC-2, but none of the tests came back with the virus. Nothing. We tried to find it because it had all the telltale symptoms of ARC," he explained. "I thought another strain emerged, one we couldn't see. I was contacted immediately. Nothing we tried worked, and unlike when you had ARC, it progressed rapidly. We've been seeing this for a good year."

"A year?"

"A year,' he repeated. "I am simply devastated Travis."

"Richard, what is going on?" I asked.

"This is me. This is my arrogance, I caused this. There are not seventeen thousand people, there are a lot more.":

"How are you responsible for a virus?" I asked,

"It's not a virus. It's the effects of the vaccine."

The phone nearly fell from my hand. "What?"

"We created the vaccine using a manmade, super targeting, Activity Regulator Cytoskeleton protein. It acted as a barrier, working with the ARC gene, protecting the brain from degenerative disease. What we didn't expect or think would happen, is the gene would start rejecting it, and in turn, eventually, caused the opposite effect. Instead of protecting the brain, it broke it down. Rapid degenerative brain disease."

"What about another vaccine?" I asked. "I'm not a scientist, but can't we toss that super protein at it."

"Oh, we tried that," Richard said. "The results were even more devastating."

"What does all this mean, Richard? What is happening?"

"Just imagine the stages of Alzheimer's progressing at a rapid rate."

"How rapid?" I asked,

"Start to finish ... at the most, weeks. We saw one case last just about a month. That was it. Fastest a couple days. Usually accidents have been the cause."

"Jesus, Richard, I'm sorry."

"No, I'm sorry," he said. "Eventually everyone is going to know the truth. We celebrated this cure, we were proud of it. Five point three billion people, men, women and children received the vaccination, and in two weeks, five point three billion people won't even know their name."

It was like an earthquake inside my being, the shaking rumbled in my belly, and caused my heart to pound. I stumbled back and sat down, barely able to catch my breath. "Everyone?" I asked. "Everyone that got it? That can't be right. You have to be wrong. It can't be right."

"I have to go."

"Richard, tell me what we can do?"

"Go get your wife, Travis, bring her home."

"And?"

"Bring her home. She doesn't have much time."

Click.

That was it. He ended the call, leaving me reeling in his news that didn't make sense and I didn't fully understand. Billions of people got that vaccination, was he really saying that billions of people would be like my wife?

Like an idiot, I screamed his name over and over in the phone. I wanted to slam the phone on the counter. Instead, I growled in angry frustration.

"Dad?" Beau called my name. "You okay?"

I pursed my lips trying to control my emotions. "Um, yeah." I looked at my son holding my daughter's hand and that was when the most heartbreaking thought hit me.

My wife wasn't the only one who received the vaccine. Our children did, too.

EIGHT – DRAWING

February 19

There is a certain amount of deniability when faced with horrific news. It was a strange process I went through. To me there was no way this was going to reach some sort of biblical proportion.

If Richard was right and it was those who received the vaccine, I was doomed to live and watch my family suffer.

In the four days since we brought Maranda home, she grew worse. She remembered less, was often confused, and we had to watch her carefully and constantly.

It was nothing compared to the stories I was seeing on the news.

I didn't want to watch the news, but I was drawn to it.

There was no hiding the story, downplaying it, they couldn't.

"So you think it can be stopped," the newscaster asked some scientist.

"We think we can, unfortunately, for too many Americans it will be too late. We're not looking at a gradual process like most degenerative brain diseases, we are looking at a quick onset and a launch into a late stage. The protein turned into a predator and the brain is the prey."

I hated listening to the news, but I had to hold on to hope, wait to hear something that could give me encouragement for my family.

The ravaging effects couldn't be downplayed or ignored,

two-hundred and sixty-four million Americans alone received the vaccine.

My question was, if they were progressing or would progress like Maranda, who was going to take care of them. How many people would wander aimlessly on the street, not knowing who they were, how to dress, eat or to even recognize danger.

Those were the confused ones.

There were those who had outbursts with little provocation, and some went catatonic.

The day after I brought Maranda home, health authorities talked about a 'plan', but didn't say specifically what it was. But through what little they did say, they expressed what I was thinking.

Bottom line, there weren't enough healthy to care for the ones that were going to get ill.

If they couldn't be saved, what about their quality of life?

As it stood, everyone would be a caretaker until they could no longer take care of themselves.

Then what?

I hadn't been to work in a week, and it was days since I had even left the house. I needed things from the store. I needed to feed my kids. This meant leaving them alone. Alone with Maranda.

It would be fine, at least just for Beau. He would be there in case something went wrong. And it was possible. Three times since she had been home, Maranda wandered. from the apartment, down the stairs and to the street. In her bare feet. No coat. She tried to make tea on the stove and didn't put water in the pot.

Hating to do it, for when we slept or, had to leave, the day before I had resorted to not only putting locks on the bedroom window, but an exterior lock on the door. My poor wife was a prisoner of not only her mind, but in her home.

I decided to take Daisy with me to the store, less burden and worry on my young son. I secured Maranda in her room and just told him to let me know if anything went wrong. I would be back. We would walk to Dewalt's. It would be a lot faster to walk the two blocks than clearing the snow from the truck and finding a parking spot for just a couple bags we could tote ourselves.

Plus, it would be good to get Daisy out of the house.

The temperatures weren't frigid, the sun peaked through a little and it was in that stage of winter warm just before another snowfall.

Still, I bundled her up and we left the apartment.

As we stepped from the building, Daisy stopped to look in the gallery. I held her hand seeing our reflection in the glass.

"Daddy, do you think Mommy can still paint?" she asked.

"I don't know."

"Maybe she should try." Daisy looked up at me with those big innocent eyes. Something about her suggestion clicked.

Maybe the creativity was instinctual. What would happen if I gave her a canvas and brushes?

"You know what Daisy, I think that's a great idea."

Turning from the gallery, I saw him approach from behind.

Chief Fisher.

"Good to see you out, Travis," he said. "How's Maranda?"

"Same. Not ... better." I glanced down to Daisy. "We're headed to the store right now."

"What store?"

I smiled. "Dewalt's."

"It's closed, Travis," the Chief said. "They closed yesterday. If you need something, I have access. I'm trying right now to set up a schedule."

"Why did Eddie close?"

"His wife did. Eddie ... Eddie is like Maranda along with at least forty other people in town."

"Oh my God."

"You haven't been out Travis, things are going downhill fast."

"I've been so preoccupied with Maranda," I said.

"I understand. I wanted to stop by and talk to you," the Chief said. "Will you be around this evening?"

"Sure, what's going on?"

"I got a memo from the state, they tried to reach out to you. Emailed, called, and even sent you a social media message."

I shook my head. "I haven't bothered with any of that. Why are they looking for me?"

"Because you and I are two of twelve people in town that didn't get the Vaccine."

"Okay," I said confused.

"You can say it's a call to arms."

I was trying to register what he meant. Like we were getting called to some sort of war?

"If you'll excuse me," the Chief said. "I'll be by later." He extended his hand, touching Daisy's face. "You be good and help Daddy."

"I will," Daisy replied.

"See you in a little while, Travis." The chief walked away.

"Daddy are we still going to the store?" Daisy asked.

"I don't think so sweetie. Looks like I'm gonna have to take some of that California Bologns out of the freezer." Holding her hand I turned to take her back in. Then I thought, maybe just a little longer, I'd keep her out. She needed to get out of the apartment.

I was ready to tell her that we were going to take a little walk down the street, when I looked at the gallery.

"You know what, Daisy? You had such a good idea before. What do you say we go in mom's gallery and get her some stuff to make a painting?"

"Okay," Daisy replied brightly.

I pulled the keys out of my back pocket, fiddled to find the correct one and then I unlocked the gallery door.

We stepped in. It was dark in there and I immediately turned on all the lights. The overhead, the tracking. I illuminated all of her paintings and they were painful to see.

Daisy's voice trailed as she ran toward the back. "I'm gonna grab her paint brushes and paint."

"I'll be right there to get the canvas." I told her, pausing at one of my wife's paintings. Maranda's soul was stamped on every creation. She left her mark. It broke my heart to think she would never do another, and if she did, would she even know? She had reached the point where she didn't remember eating, struggled to know my name and more often than not kept asking who Beau was.

Maybe something about the art would bring her back, even just for a moment.

"Daddy, how many colors should I get," Daisy hollered from the back.

"Get a bunch baby, she can mix," I replied. "I'll be right ... there." On my last word I watched the blue sedan fly down the snow covered street.

My body turning in shock, seeing it fly by the window and thinking, "They must have an emergency," only to learn quickly my thinking was wrong when I heard the crash.

It caused me to jump, and I instinctively reached for the door.

"Daisy!" I shouted. "Stay here. Don't leave." I flung open the gallery door. That same car had slammed right into Hot Box Pizza. The front end of the car smashed against the corner of the building. No attempts to stop. Steam flowed from the engine, clearly the air bags deployed and the windshield was shattered.

I ran to help the driver, and saw Chief Fisher was arriving before me.

Surely the driver was hurt, there was no way he or she wasn't.

Then the driver's door opened, and the driver, a man about my age, stepped out.

Blood poured down his face, his legs were wobbly, and he staggered from the car.

"Hold on, just hold on," Fisher said to the man. "You're hurt."

But the man said nothing, he walked right by the Chief, running his hand on the car as a means of support. He walked around the back of the car, leaving a trail of blood as he went straight to the door of the pizza shop.

Anyone that was in the pizza shop was already outside. They had run out when they heard the crash and no doubt, felt the jolt.

A Hot Box pizza worker in a blue shirt, tried to stop the man. "You can't go in."

"I just want my pizza. I want my pizza."

"Sir, you need medical help."

The man seriously injured, standing and reacting on memory, felt no pain. Just like George felt nothing.

Unlike George, the man reacted verbally. He yelled at the employee, screaming about his pizza.

Chief Fisher tried to calm him, but the man was enraged.

He reminded me of Eddie Dewalt when he was young and stupid. Eddie liked to drink, but he was an angry drunk and would act unreasonably and throw a tantrum in a drunk rage when he did anything wrong.

That was not the case here.

The man, like my wife and so many others, had lost his mind, his reasoning and thought processes were gone.

It was a frightening vision of what was to come.

I couldn't, nor did I want to, envision what the world was going to be like when eighty percent of the world became like my wife and this man.

<><><><>

Nothing.

There was nothing there. No moment of familiarity, happiness, knowing. Maranda looked at me with wonder, or maybe as if I were nuts giving her something she had no idea how to use. It was like giving someone a car they didn't know how to drive.

"It's there," I told her. "It's in your heart. Try. To. Find it."

I knew my words of encouragement were short.

"You're a nice man," she said. "Can you tell my mother where

I am?"

"Yeah, I will."

Her mother had passed away years ago.

Seeing her, I inwardly fought the knowledge that what happened to her was going to happen to everyone that got the vaccine.

I talked to my children, asked them questions, hoping not to see signs it had hit them as well.

But what were the signs? How early were the warnings? Not very. Everything I read, it just happened so fast.

I didn't lock the bedroom door, I hated doing that. Instead, I double bolted the apartment door and placed a chair before it with pots and pans. An alarm of sorts should she try to get out.

The kids had to eat, and I had to figure out what to make them.

Beau sat at the kitchen table, pen in hand. He was writing or drawing something, I wasn't really sure what and didn't look. I patted him on the back in a gentle way, then opened the freezer to see what we had in there.

When I reached for the handle, I saw it.

The business card I was given that day at Reilly's. I don't know why I didn't think about it, that day was a blur that seemed to start it all. Before examining the freezer, I slipped the card from under the magnet.

"Be right back Beau, I have to make a call." I made my way down the hall and peeked in on Daisy in the playroom.

"Hi Daddy did you take the California Bologns out of the freezer?" She looked up from her dolls.

"I will, Daddy needs to make a call first. Stay in here."

"Okay."

I pulled out my phone, I really didn't expect him to answer. After all, not only was he a doctor, but I was a completely unknown number to him. I thought in my head what I'd say to his voice mail and once I knew, I dialed the number and headed to the living room... To my surprise, he answered.

"This is Doctor Yee."

"Oh my gosh, I was not expecting you to answer at all."

"You called. What did you expect?" he asked.

"A voicemail."

"You got me. What can I help you with sir?" he asked.

"I'm a little rattled, I wasn't expecting to talk to you yet."

"Why don't you just say what you were gonna say on the voicemail," he said.

"Okay." I cleared my throat. "Hey, Doctor Yee. This is Travis Grady. We met at a restaurant a few days back where George dipped his arm in grease. Anyhow ..."

"Stop," Doctor Yee said. 'I remember you well. You don't forget people you meet under such extenuating circumstances. What's up, Travis?"

"I don't know how it is out your way, Doc, but out here, it's getting bad."

"With the reaction."

"To the vaccine, yes," I replied.

"It's bad everywhere Travis. Every day millions are falling to this."

"That just seems so, I don't know, farfetched doesn't it?" I asked.

"I wish it was farfetched, but it's happening."

"The reason I called is, you mentioned this Eastern medicine. My wife ... my wife is ..."

"One of The Lost. That's what I call them. Lost. It's called the Lost Effect. I'm sorry to hear that. You have children, right? How are they."

"Good so far, thank God."

"You?" he asked.

"I'm fine. Nothing is happening to me. Like you I didn't get the vaccine, in fact, I'm one of the Great Eight, as they called us."

"Wow, that's pretty big. So like me, you're destined to be witness to it all going down."

"I hate it. And I feel guilty," I said. "I mean I was part of it."

"You can't look at it that way, Travis. That was a couple years ago. How many people got real time with loved ones they would have lost?"

"Now everyone is gonna lose. Including me. My wife."

"I am really sorry. How far is she?" he asked.

"It's pretty bad. I mean a few days ago she was slipping, now she doesn't know us and ..." I dropped my voice to a whisper. "She can't even go to the bathroom on her own. Man, if she was aware it would kill her. Is there anything we can do?"

"Unfortunately, you can not undo the damage," he said. "Remember when the vaccine was first given to Alzheimer's and other dementia sufferers. Some damage was too far progressed, and some it just kinda halted the damage done. No one returned to normal because the brain just doesn't heal like that."

"But if we found something to stop it, she wouldn't digress?" I asked.

"I can't say, Travis."

"I'm not a scientist, but what if we give them the vaccine again. Like you said it halted the damage ..."

"Travis," he stopped me. "To me that's a brilliant idea and when a friend and fellow colleague said the same thing two days ago, I said go for it. His wife, and others he knew that showed symptoms of the Lost Effect, he got them to take the vaccine. We all thought, heck, what is there to lose?"

"And?" I asked.

"And we found out what there was to lose. Days."

"I'm sorry."

"Precious days. One more day to say I love you, to see them, to hear them. Those were gone. The vaccine jet streamed it to the final stage."

"Which is?"

"The brain forgets how to walk, talk, swallow and ... eventually breathe."

"What if we try it again," I suggested.

"You can try. Find the town doctor, try, but be prepared to lose her quickly."

I sighed out heavily, I know he heard it.

"Look, I understand what you're going through. You don't

want to give up, you want to try everything. If I had a wife and kids, I'd be the same way. No one is telling you to stop trying."

"What is everyone doing for The Lost there?" I asked.

"Doing our best to make them comfortable and take care of them."

"Can I call you if I have questions?" I asked. "I mean, you can tell me no. I can text ..."

"Call me anytime."

"One more question, Doc. Will my wife hit that last phase where it all just stops?"

"I'm sorry to say," he replied. "Everyone does."

I thanked him again, promising to call him and vice versa, then I hung up, checked on Daisy again and went back to the kitchen.

"Okay." I grabbed the freezer door. "Sorry we couldn't go to the store. Let's see what we have. Daisy wants that California Bologns, I think this is chicken." I grabbed a pack of meat. "Not sure. What do you think, Bud? What are you in the mood for?" I glanced over at Beau and his hand moved frantically on the paper. "Man, you are working hard on something." I stepped to the table. "What are you ...."

Beau never stopped. His hand went back and forth, up and down on that paper like a mad sketch artist. He kept going, staring down, not listening, not responding. If his reaction didn't crush me and tell me enough, the paper did. My son wasn't drawing anything but scratches, scribbles and lines.

NINE – DUTY

The shed door, clasp latch I picked up at the hardware store came in a set of two, and I never thought I would have to use both in my own home.

The metal loop of the padlock rested on my index finger and I stared at it, tapping the lock, causing a slight swing as I wallowed in my own self-pity and grief on my living room sofa.

I was blindsided by Beau. No other signs, I didn't see it coming at all. But then I had to think, when was the last time I heard him speak? Did he speak to me at all when I left with Daisy for our short trip to the store?

While he sat at that table drawing savagely, I called his name, sat next to him, begged for his attention, it went on for ten minutes. Even when his pencil shredded the paper and he was drawing on the surface of the table ... nothing.

Then finally, he just stopped, slowly looked at me and said, "I'm going to be late for school."

I told him he wasn't and he argued with me until he stopped and he went to his room.

I locked his windows, not his door.

There was no doctor to call, no help to be given, at least none that I knew of, and I had searched. I watched the news, went on line, social media, no where did it say 'seek medical attention'. In fact, the major news network had only recently started stating what some experts were saying to do.

"It's difficult when multiple members of families are being lost to this," the newswoman said. "Is there anything they can do?"

I saw the so called expert come on, a man I had seen many

times over the past few days, there wasn't much more or anything different I thought could come from his mouth.

He was encouraging people not to break the delusion. Because he was seeing violent reactions to being contradicted.

I stood in the middle of his 'we all have to work together, help each other' speech and walked to the window.

Work together? Help each other? How? My family had me, but what about the millions of families that would all fall to The Lost category together? Who would help them?

I looked out the window to the main street. It had snowed again, but there were no tire tracks, no plow marks. In fact, it was hard to see, a thick smoke lingered in the air. Not only did the street lights give them a weird lighting effect, there was an orange hue to things.

That could only mean one thing. A fire. It was close, but I hadn't heard any sirens. It hit me fires could be something that would happen a lot more. The inability of The Lost to know what they were doing.

I felt so defeated and devastated, my gut held on to this sinking feeling and I was waiting for the next ax to drop, shoe to fall, family member to be lost.

My daughter. She was next.

I hadn't heard from my sister or brother-in-law, even though I reached out to them three times.

I couldn't even leave my family to go check on them.

"If you're just joining us," the newswoman said. "Richard Collins ...."

Hearing Richard's name drew my attention from that window.

Instantly I thought, maybe he came up with a solution, I was hopeful, and then I heard the newswoman.

"The famed epidemiologist that created the Alzheimer vaccine, has died."

"What?" I blasted the television.

"The doctor who has been blamed for everything that is happening, took his own life this afternoon in his Baltimore home. His wife released a statement stating, 'He was only trying to help the world and did not take his life because of recent events, but rather because he wanted to go out on his own terms knowing what he loved and who he loved.' Doctor Collins was exhibiting signs of The Lost. There was great ..."

I did and didn't want to hear more, but the newswoman gave me no choice. She tilted her head as if someone were talking to her and said nothing.

The blank stare, the instant lost expression. Her lips moving in a hopeless silent stutter. It was like that on camera for the world to see. Then a crew member rushed forward and the screen went to color bars and a mid-pitched tone.

I grabbed the remote to turn it off and the knock at my door startled me.

It was late, but I kind of knew who it was. I carefully moved my chair with the pots and unlocked the door.

"Hey, Travis," Chief Fisher said. "Sorry for being so late. I saw the light on."

"It's fine, come on in." I opened the door wider for him.

When he stepped inside, he looked down at the pots and pans. "Cooking in the hall."

"It's my alarm system. If the door opens, I'll hear."

"That's a good idea. I have an old bell at the station, if you want."

"I may take you up on it."

"How is she?" he asked.

"They," I corrected.

"Oh, Travis, I'm sorry."

"Yeah, my boy ... he well, he went into the zone pretty fast."

"Where are they now?"

"Sleeping."

"You're lucky," the Chief said. "A lot of people can't get family members to sleep."

"I cheated. I gave them nighttime cough medicine. Maybe it's not right, but I can't care for them if I don't rest."

Chief Fisher sighed out, lowering his head and lifting his

eyes to me.

“What is it?” I asked.

“Travis, it’s been a hell of a night. Seven car crashes, two fires. In the course of one day, we went from forty people with this to half the town.”

“How? How is it happening so fast?”

Chief Fisher shrugged. “I don’t know. My guess is the order they got the vaccination. Just a guess. But me and the others like us, we’re trying, and I got an automated call, apparently state is setting something up. Fortunately, they are using those who didn’t get the virus, so it will get to us.”

“What?”

“Help, I guess, who knows? But, Travis, we need help. I know you are here with your family, but there are so many out there. They can’t take care of themselves, not eating, wandering, they’re a danger. They keep getting into cars and …”

“I hear you,” I said. “I do. I hear you. I can’t leave my family to take care of strangers.”

“I understand. Just thought I’d try,” Chief Fisher said. “None of us want to, you know. We all have family elsewhere that we want to get to, but we’re here. Will you think about it?”

“Chief, I …”

“You have friends in this town, what about them?” the Chief pressed.

“I just …” I looked over my shoulder.

“Travis, how about this …” Chief Fisher paused in the door. “What would you want someone to do for your family? What if you weren’t here? What would happen to them if someone didn’t sacrifice to help? That’s all I’m gonna say. Have a good night.” He nodded, walked out the door and closed it.

As much as I wanted to help others, I couldn’t. I just couldn’t. My family needed me.

TEN – NO DIRECTION

February 20

The lights were still on, we had power and that was a blessing. Considering half the town was lost, it begged to question, who was manning the power stations? Eventually it would stop, I hoped at least the weather wasn't as cold or snowy. We had been pounded by snow.

I couldn't remember the last time that happened.

I woke up on the couch wanting things to be normal again. It would have been eerily quiet had it not been for the music coming from Daisy's room. That was the only bright spot when reality smacked me in the face when I woke up. She played music in her room all the time. Whether it was some silly children's song or something completely left field, she went into her room and listened.

When we remodeled our building, we had created a two story apartment, but more so the bedrooms on the upper floor were loft style, that was where the kids were.

The second floor could be seen from the living room. The high railings we placed around the hallway. I went up to check and peeked in on Daisy, she was twirling around, still in her pajamas. That was good, I needed her to stay there in her safe world. Not see what else was going on.

I hadn't put the lock on Beau's door and it scared me when I didn't see him, until I realized he was the one in the bathroom.

"Hey, Bud, you okay?" I asked, knocking on the bathroom door.

"Just getting ready for school," he replied.

He sounded like himself, and that was a good thing.

"You don't have school today," I told him.

"I have school."

"No, Bud, it's a snow day. I'm gonna go help your mom then I'll get breakfast."

I really needed some coffee and put a pot on, then listened to the door of my bedroom to see if I heard Maranda.

She was quiet, probably still asleep. Beau was taking a while in the bathroom and I checked on him again before the pot had even brewed.

He was fine, still claiming to be getting ready for school, so I poured a cup, took a few sips and grabbed some juice for Maranda.

It took me a second to compose myself, hating myself for locking her in like a prisoner. I set the orange juice on the floor by the door while I undid the lock.

The bed was slightly messed up, but I suspected she slept in the chair.

When I walked in she stared out the window. I set the juice on the dresser.

"It snowing," she said, no emotion, no feeling.

"A lot. Again." I walked to the window and took her arm, I suspected as I had for the last couple mornings, I'd have to help her to the bathroom. She didn't argue, only questioning once if she needed to go.

I assured her she did, aided in what I could then led her back to the bedroom.

"Sit down, I'll be right back." I returned to the bathroom and while the water ran in a cycle to get warm, I dampened her tooth brush, placed some paste on it, and filled a glass. I took that out, setting it on the night stand, then returned to put soap on a wash cloth and grab a towel.

She stared at me while I washed her face and neck, then her hands.

"Is my husband coming?" she asked.

I felt my heart sink to my stomach. "Yeah, he is. He loves you. You know that right?"

"Does he?"

"He does."

"Who are you?"

"A friend." When I finished giving her a quick wash, I handed her the toothbrush. Wrapping my fingers around hers, I brought it to her mouth and initiated the motion. Once I saw she had it, I took the towels back to the bathroom and grabbed the waste paper basket. "Here you go." I removed the toothbrush from her hand. "Spit."

It took a second, staring from me to the can. I had to mock show her. When she leaned her over the basket, I heard it. A frightening sound, the clanking of pots and pans.

My homemade door alarm.

"Shit." I stepped back and she grabbed me wrist.

"Where are you going?"

"I have to go. I'll be right back."

"No don't go." Her fingers locked tightly into my skin, exhibiting strength that I didn't know she had. Her face was frightened, almost matching the feel of panic I had boiling in me. I peeled her fingers from my arm, and raced out the bedroom door.

The sound pots and pans falling could only mean one thing.

One of my children had left.

"Daddy?" Daisy called my name. "I tried to stop him."

I felt the cold air hit me the second I made it to the front hall. The door was open. I didn't grab my coat, just shoved my feet into my boots without tying them, then barreled down the stairs.

He couldn't be far? It was only a minute or two.

How wrong I was.

I stepped out into the deep snow, the blustering wind pelting me with the hard falling flakes. It was a near white out. Running out into the street, I looked left and right. My inner being shook with a panic I had never felt before. Standing there in the middle of the barren street, I screamed out my loudest, "Beau!"

I swore the only person that didn't hear me calling for my son was … my son. Three people meandered to the sidewalk, but most looked at me like I was nuts, like I didn't know what I was doing.

There was a brief moment, not the first nor the last, I doubted my own sanity.

Were they looking at me as if I were one of The Lost? Was I? Had I lost my mind? I wondered, the way they looked at me, didn't say anything.

I couldn't worry about them. I stood there in the street yelling for Beau. I didn't know what to do. I wanted to run and start searching, I had a feeling where he may have gone. I needed a coat, but didn't want to leave the street in case he came back and I couldn't leave Daisy alone with Maranda.

I panicked, felt overwhelmed and even thought for a split second I was over reacting.

Just stop. Breathe. Think about it. I knew I had to make choices when Maranda stepped outside wearing only her nightgown.

Like a child, she turned in circles tilting her face to the falling flakes and smiling.

I was mortified and just didn't know what to do.

It took everything I had not to scream. I had to get it together.

I rushed to Maranda, "You need to get inside."

"Isn't it beautiful."

"Please get inside."

"What are you doing?" Maranda asked me.

"Beau ran off."

"Who?" she asked.

I closed my eyes, taking a second, trying again, to keep it together.

"Travis?" I heard the woman's voice call my name, seeping through the wind.

One hand, still holding on to Maranda, I turned, looking over my shoulder to see my neighbor, Terri.

"Hold on," she hollered, holding up a finger as if to tell me to wait. She lived across the street, and like us, occupied an apartment above her store, Meehan Used Books. It was obvious she had rushed out. Her winter coat was half on. One sleeve dangled, nearly tripping her as she wrangled the wandering Lost, like a preschool teacher grabbing toddlers, ushering them back into her bookstore. She closed the door and placed a chair in front to keep them in. Then placing on her coat the rest of the way, she made her way toward me.

I was surprised to see her, a couple days earlier, I swore I saw her packing her car. As she drew close, I saw she looked as exhausted as I felt. The snow landed on her short dark hair, plastering it to her head.

"Travis, what's going on?" she asked. "Are you okay?"

"Yes. No," I said desperately. "Beau took off. I ... I have to look for him. I can't leave, Maranda. She's ... she's ..."

Terri cased Maranda and drew a sympathetic look. "Lost?"

"Yes."

"Daisy?"

"She's fine. For now. I can't leave, I can't go. I have to find my son."

"Travis, I can't stay here, I'm taking care of people, but if you want, you can bring Maranda to me. I'll keep her while you look," she said.

"Daisy?"

"I could use her help."

"Thank you. Thank you so much." I reached out, grabbing her shoulders. "Thank you."

"It's okay. Just get her some shoes," Terri said.

I glanced down and looked at Maranda's bare feet sinking in the snow. "I will. I'll be right over. Thank you again."

Feeling a little better, slightly calmer, I led Maranda into the building. I just had to quickly get her dressed, get Daisy, then I could go and find my son.

<><><><>

"Daddy, why are we going to the bookstore?" Daisy asked, holding my hand as we made our way down the stairs. "Does Mommy want to read?"

"Sweetie, I have to go look for Beau. Ms. Terri is going to watch Mommy because Mommy is sick." I opened the front door and led Daisy and Maranda outside. "You'll help her."

"Okay, Daddy."

Maranda moved slowly, totally mesmerized by the snow, I had to hurry her, too much time had already been lost. Even though I had a good idea where Beau had gone, I still needed to hurry. I didn't know if he had on a coat or even shoes.

There was a certain hard reality that hit me when I stepped inside the bookstore. The lights were low and mainly only the light of day lit the store.

Neighbors I had known from seeing, talking to, were there. Some wandered looking at books, others just sat, staring out.

I guess Terri noticed my surprise when I walked in.

"I'll take her. Go look for your son," Terri said.

"How many ... how many people are you taking care of here?" I asked.

"Nine."

"Nine?" I replied in shock. "That's a lot."

"Not as many as Mr. Matthews from the bank," she said. "But I guess we handle what we can. I was headed to find my parents in Ohio ... then I just ..." she sighed out. "We all have to do our part, right?"

I couldn't even say 'right' or agree, because 'my part' wasn't more than my family and that was all I could handle.

I apologized for adding more to her burden, thanked her again, then I left.

The snow had let up some, but the street and sidewalks were covered with a fresh layer.

There were tire tracks and worst of all, there were no footprints other than the ones we just made.

There was no indication what direction Beau had gone, and to find him, I just had to follow my instinct.

ELEVEN – DROPLETS IN THE SNOW

My first thought was that there was no way, no possible way that Beau could have made it to the middle school. Even though it was only a mile and a half, he wasn't out there long enough to make it that far on foot, especially in the snow. But I had to try. After all, he was insistent he had class, it only made sense that was where he'd go.

I had only made it three blocks before I saw the flashing lights of the police car parked on the side of the road by a pickup truck with Joe Randal. It looked like Joe was dressed for the artic, heavy parka style coat with dark glasses, as he stood by the back end of his truck.

My heart took a nose dive to my gut, and immediately I thought the worst when Chief Fisher waved me down.

Please, no. Please no, I thought.

I wound down my window.

"What's going on Chief?" I asked, nervously.

"Hey, Travis, where are you headed? Didn't think I'd see you out on the roads."

"I um ... Beau took off. I don't know where he went. Have you seen him?"

"Not in this area, we just got back here a couple minutes ago."

"Have you seen any footprints?"

"Travis, there are lots of footprints around here. Lots of folks wandering," he said. "Which is why I am gonna ask you not to drive."

"I have to," I replied. "I have to get to the school. He was saying this morning he had school."

"I get that. I do. We'll even help you look, but I can't have you driving. Heck, we stopped driving an hour ago. Been walking around."

"I don't understand," I said. "I need to go. I need to look and look fast."

"I get that. Can you do it walking?"

"Why can't I drive?" I asked.

"Because, Travis, there are bodies under the snow. We're gathering them."

All the air escaped my lungs and I found it hard to even inhale.

"I don't know why," he continued. "But a lot of folks were drawn to leaving, walking out. Maybe they instinctively, like your boy, thought they had to go somewhere. Most of the people we're finding weren't wearing coats or shoes."

Immediately I thought of how my son was out in the snow, just like the others. "I'll not drive." I wound up the window and turned off the ignition. I grabbed my gloves, the blanket, and flashlight and opened the door.

"I appreciate it," the Chief said. "And we will look for Beau."

"I think he went to the school." I placed on my gloves. "Chief, how ... how is this happening? How are these people out here?"

"You were watching your son and he's out here," the Chief answered. "Imagine how many people have no one to keep them safe, feed them, it's tragic. I'm at a loss. There's not many of us still standing."

If he meant to layer on the guilt because I was able bodied, it was working. Him, Terri, Joe Randal, they were all doing what they could. I wanted to, I really did. Maybe I had to rethink things, work it out that I could help as well. But at that moment, there was nothing I could do but leave my truck and look for my son.

To me, there was always something dismal about the snow. No matter how beautiful it was, unless it was Christmas morning, the snow blanketed the world in a cold silence, burying all signs of life beneath it.

That was what it seemed to do in my town.

Nothing grew beneath the blanket of white, it was a part of the cycle of life. Birth, grow, live ... die.

Like the flowers and the grass, the snow in High Water buried the living.

Not only had twisted science taken from the life they had, knew and loved, the cold was taking their last breath.

This was not the world any of us envisioned. When I was a youngster, the end times, apocalypse would happen with a bang. Bombs, meteors, even zombies weren't quiet. But this ... this was torture, the existence of mankind slowly rolling out into extinction with a whimper.

The idea that it was 'God's End' hadn't crossed my mind. Having come from decades of Sunday school, bible studies, a preacher grandfather and heavy handed 'God says' household, I knew what the Bible said about the end. Book of Revelation, yeah there were plagues, but a whole bunch of other stuff that was like nothing we looked at.

I hadn't entertained it, in fact, dismissed it, mainly because I let go of that style of life and belief, and it hadn't crossed my mind until I passed Saint Peter's Episcopal Church a half mile from the school.

The old fashioned, one steeple white building sat on a corner lot. The Pastor was out front shoveling snow from the steps. I paused to wave and ask if he had seen Beau, when I noticed the sign.

It read.

Pray.

The Rapture is among us.

The rapture wasn't in the Book of Revelation, it was in Paul, and while interpretation had it lifting up people, body and soul, to heaven, Paul used the Greek word for 'snatched', people were 'snatched' away.

For a brief moment, reading the sign, I wonder if that indeed what was happening. Maybe God had said enough of man messing with nature and in His own way snatched the 'faithful', those who believed in the vaccine.

Snatched them.

Even though physically they were with us, they were gone.

"Are you lost?" asked the pastor, now standing not far from me.

I suppose it was his way to get a reaction, to see what I did or said.

I shook my head. "No, Reverend. I'm actually looking for my son. Have you seen a boy, thirteen around?"

"Sorry, son, I haven't. Is he ... Lost?"

"He is."

"I'm sorry."

"I'll find him."

"I'll pray for you," he said.

"I appreciate it." I started to leave and stopped. "Reverend, your sign. Do you believe that?"

"I put it there, didn't I?" he replied.

"Yeah, but do you believe it?"

"I don't know." The reverend placed his hands on the shovel handle. "I don't. I suppose I put it there for me and others. To me it's easier and more comforting to believe that God is behind this. That our loved ones are in a better place. That they're already gone and their body is going through the motions."

"How is that easier to believe?" I asked.

"Because the alternative, the scientific explanation is worse. If God didn't do this, if God hasn't already pulled them out of their bodies and put them in a better place," he said, "Then right now, all those Lost, are truly in a living hell. And we are right along with them."

How true his words, but sadly, science and man caused this.

It was hell.

The only comfort in it all was hoping that those like Maranda just didn't know.

I moved on, realizing I had been out for over an hour. The phones were still working, and I called the chief. A fear of mine was Beau returning home and no one was there.

He assured me he had someone watching and checking, yet no sign of Beau.

I turned the bend from the church on to Garden Boulevard, four lane road north of town where I'd find the school. There were slightly, snowed over tire tracks on the road, the first I had seen since I left the Chief. They weren't that old and not much snow had filled them in.

They moved recklessly, and I wondered if it was the slipperiness of the road or perhaps a wayward Lost driver.

I followed the tracks and finally made it to the school. The tire tracks kept going, but I didn't. I just knew by looking at the front that he wasn't there. It was dark, the staircase was completely covered with snow, so much so it looked like a hillside. No indentations at all from footprints. No one had been in the school since before the first heavy snow had fallen.

But I was there. I had to check anyhow.

The snow came nearly to my knee as I attempted the steps slowly, feeling for the next rise, I knew there to be at least ten steps.

There were three sets of double metal doors at the entrance. I tried the center ones first … nothing. But the set to the right was unlocked and I went inside.

The bang of the closing door, echoed in the hollow hallways. I turned my flashlight on to brighten the way and called out, "Beau! Beau, you here?"

My own voice bounced back at me. I looked on the floor for wet footprints. Surely, if Beau was there, he would had entered through the front doors.

I was wasting time and I knew it. I turned to leave when I

heard a sound.

A faint banging. It was steady. A bang, a few seconds and a bang again. My boots squeaked on the linoleum as I spun around and raced toward the sound.

Rounding the bend, my boots squeaked again on the floor when I came to a grinding halt. It wasn't my son. It was the school janitor. In a repeat motion, holding on to his cleaning cart, he pushed forward, the cart hit the wall, he'd bounce back and try again only to hit that wall.

I didn't bother calling out. I knew, he like almost everyone ... was Lost.

Defeated, I turned and left the school. I tried to follow my own footprints down the stairs, but it was still slick.

"Beau! Beau!" I yelled my loudest making my way to the street. "Beau!" I turned left then right.

Where was my son?

I took a deep breath to call out again, and that was when I saw it. Or at least I thought I did. Had I not been looking, I would have missed it. Twenty feet or so past the school, closer to the sidewalk was a dark spot. Was it a shoe? A bag. Something was in the snow.

I ran to the spot, crouched down for it and saw it was a book. A big, thick book. I would have pulled it out of the snow had I not noticed the pattern in the snow that formed right by it. It reminded of the time that Maranda was frustrated and flung the paint from her brush on to the white canvas. Only this splatter wasn't blue, it was red.

Deep red.

Blood.

And like any splashed paint, drops scattered.

In the snow, blood droplets created a treasure map dashed line, leading me to the embankment on the side of the road where I saw part of a bare foot protruding from the mound.

"No, no, no." I rushed over to the snow and immediately my hands dug through. "No, no. Please no."

My hands paddled through fast and furiously with each inch

of snow more drenched with blood than the previous.

A leg. A bloody bare leg was uncovered next.

In the ice cold weather, I felt the burning heat of emotions take over me. I prayed, my God, I prayed with all my heart that the body I discovered was not my son. To let it be one of the countless wandering souls of town that froze in the bitter cold weather.

It didn't take long for me to discover it wasn't a neighbor or stranger, it was my son.

A sickening feeling filled my gut as I pulled my son out of his bloody, snowy entombment. His body only cold from the weather, the blood still fresh. I frantically searched for a pulse, but there was none.

Curling him into my chest, my knees dug deep into the snow, I gut screamed as loud as I could, as I cradled my son against me.

No amount of screaming could release the pain I felt in my body and soul,

Holding him, I saw flashes of his life.

His birth, first step, infatuation with wrestling. I saw the life he would never have, to grow up, love, have a family.

Paralyzed in pain, I was crushed. My son, my first born ... was gone.

<><><><>

The driver of the car was dead.

Good.

I didn't care.

The car was found a half mile down the road, crashed into a pole. I didn't need Chief Fisher to tell me his 'police interpretation' of what happened. I knew.

Beau was going to school. Some driver, not knowing what he was doing, or going, hit him and kept going. The intense impact not only sailed Beau to the side of the street, he landed so hard, the snow collapsed and buried him.

I saw that for myself.

The only consolation was, he probably never knew what hit him. For my son that gave an inkling of comfort, for me it did nothing,

"We'll take him," the Chief said.

"Where?" I asked.

"We're taking the bodies to Buscio's Funeral Home, keeping them there until we figure out what we're going to do."

It just seemed inconceivable to me, they were storing all the dead?

"No." I shook my head, still holding him.

"Travis, it's cold, your daughter, your wife, need you. I know you're in pain. I know this is horrible," Fisher said. "But let us take him."

"And do what? Just lump him in with everyone else?"

"Do you have a better suggestion?" The Chief asked. "Because right now, goddamn it, I'll take any suggestions. You can't stay in the street, and right now you can't even bury him. Are you even ready to bury him?"

I shook my head.

"No. Just like I am not ready to bury my nephew. We have to process what is happening. It's too fast, everything that's happening. You need to go home. Be with your family."

"He is my family." I felt his hand grip my shoulder has a showing of sympathy. "I'll take him."

"We'll all go together."

As hard as it was, I had to do it. I had to take my son from that street and get back to Maranda and Daisy. How would I tell them? I didn't have the words to explain it to myself.

The Chief helped me carry Beau to the back of Joe Randal's truck. I stayed back there with him while we drove to the funeral home. It didn't matter how cold it was, I didn't feel it. All I felt was heartache.

Pulling up to the funeral home was eerie. The large converted Victorian style house always looked spooky to me. But now, it was dark, surrounded by snow and it was obvious by the abundance of partially open windows it was being used, or at least set up to be a whole house refrigerator storage facility.

The impact of the epidemic on our town didn't hit me until I carried my son through the door. For days I watched it from my window, not being part of the town, focused only on my family.

There was no ignoring it, reality set in. Not only how much High Water was hit, but how much work Chief Fisher, Joe Randal, Pastor Monroe, Terri and the others had done.

The furniture from the viewing rooms was stacked in the hallway.

The first room to my right was completely filled, bodies lay in neat rows on the floor. Some covered, some not. When I went to the next, Chief Fisher suggested that I put Beau in the director's office where he had his nephew.

Privacy for me, to say my goodbyes when I was ready.

All those people, I felt as though I was suffocating, unable to breathe because the truth of it all was crashing down.

It took me some time to be able to leave Beau, but I knew I could come back. I knew I had to come back, I wasn't ready to say goodbye. Not yet.

I had the hurdle of facing my family. I guess Terri heard the news, because she raced out of the bookstore before I even reached for the door.

"Go home and change," she said. "You cannot let your daughter see you like this."

I didn't know what that meant, did she mean how distraught I was, until I glanced down and saw I was covered in blood.

I crossed the street, went back to my place and showered. I stood under the hot water long enough to cry, to try to get some of it out of me so I could be strong enough to tell them.

That wall I thought I put up, crumbled piece by piece every time my daughter asked. "Daddy, did you find Beau? Do you know where he is?"

I didn't know how to tell her, but I would.

Once I brought Daisy and Maranda back to the apartment, I asked Daisy to go to her room and I'd be up shortly.

I watched her go up the stairs, I tried to keep my eyes from straying and looking at Beau's room.

Maranda stood in the living room, she had this look, this smile on her face as she too watched Daisy.

Was she there? Did she know her daughter? I led her to the sofa and sat her down, grabbing her hands as I knelt before her.

"You look sad," she said.

"I am."

She tilted her head, her eyes shifting back and forth looking at me.

"Sweetheart." I squeezed her hands. "I don't know if you even know what I am saying, but ... he's gone. I went to look for him. I found him. Beau ... Beau is gone, he died."

"Oh," she softly gasped out. "I am sorry. Do I know him?"

There was a fine line for a few seconds that I clung to, trying not to cross. It was fleeting but there. An understanding for her condition and anger for her forgetting our son. But I had to understand. She didn't register it, nor did she feel it.

A part of me envied her. She would never know the crushing heartache of losing her child. She was spared that pain. It was in that moment I realized, my wife, my Maranda was truly one of The Lost, and in a sense, right there and then, in my own way, so was I.

TWELVE – MERCY ME

February 22

The smoke from the crematorium at Buscio's rose high into the sky and I could see it from my living room window. I noticed it when I looked out after hearing the loud sounds of engines.

Four large military trucks rolled down Main Street.

It was a diversion from the television that had some old school black screen and typewriter type lettering, while the emergency alert recording continuously played asking for those not affected, those not vaccinated to call a number, to give their time and help. There was something strange about an electronic voice with no emotion saying, "Humanity is tested and we must pull together to help those who cannot help themselves." Robotic and cold. Something about it I couldn't tolerate and it didn't urge me to do anything.

Perhaps it was just me. I was beginning to think it was.

The trucks though sent a different message to me.

It was the first sign of outside life I had seen in days.

Then again, the previous two days since Beau had died were a blur.

I didn't know why the trucks arrived, rolling in noisily like some sort of cavalry, but I did know the smoke from Buscio's wasn't from my son.

I had been there twice and couldn't make the call. I wanted to bury him, but the ground was frozen solid. I knew I had to make the decision soon. But I was dealing with Daisy who was devasted about Beau. She cried all the time and hadn't listened to music in two days.

I also was dealing with Maranda whose rapid decline was painful to watch. Chief Fisher told me most people didn't hold on longer than four or five days and Maranda was already at ten.

My breaking point was in reach. So many times I watched through the window as the Chief, Terri, Joe and others did their part, while I stayed home. What choice did I have?

"Daddy?"

I turned from the window to see Daisy. I was so grateful to hear my name, she was still fine and that made me happy.

"What was that noise?" she asked.

"Military trucks," I answered.

"Why are they here?"

"I don't know." I glanced again through the window then back to Daisy. "Did you want to go find out?"

Biting her bottom lip, she nodded.

"Okay, get your boots and coat," I told her. I knew she needed to get out of the apartment. We both needed it. It wasn't as cold as the previous days, the sun finally came out, melting the snow some.

Daisy rushed for her coat and boots, quickly throwing them on. I zipped her little pink coat, placed on the hood, then I grabbed my own coat.

I didn't worry about locking Maranda in the room.

She wasn't walking anywhere, not now.

We made our way out of the building, and I told my daughter, we'd follow the slushy tracks. Just as we hit the street, I saw the door to Terri's book store open and she and another man carried out a body.

There was no truck, what were they doing with it? Then I noticed several bodies, all covered, neatly lined up on the sidewalk.

Daisy's head turned that way and I hurriedly, brought her in closer to me. "Don't look, sweetie," I told her. "Keep walking. Follow the tracks."

I could have taken my truck, the snow had drifted from it

enough that clearing it wasn't a problem, and with the way the military trucks just barreled down the street, Chief Fisher's request to stay off the roads was probably lifted, but walking was good.

Daisy enjoyed it.

Following them was like going on a treasure hunt, at least for her, for me ... it worried me.

My gut instinct was confirmed when we got closer to the trucks. I heard them running, the engines were idle and loud, so they were parked.

They were parked on the street by the Municipal Building, large trucks with canvas coverings. When I saw them I thought they were bringing in equipment, until I saw the line of people on the sidewalk.

They had no belongings, some weren't wearing much more than a blanket draped over their shoulders. It looked like they were standing in a soup line, no one spoke, a lost dazed look in their eyes.

Standing across the street, I watched the situation while holding tight to my daughter's hand. From one truck they unloaded crates, a woman with a clipboard marked something down as two soldiers carried them by her to the building. She wasn't dressed as military, she wore jeans, and a flannel jacket. They didn't unload many crates, and once the final one was carried by her, she walked over to Chief Fisher. That's when I saw the people of our town led like sheep into the trucks.

"Where are they taking them, Daddy?" Daisy asked.

"I don't know. But let's find out." I lifted Daisy to my hip to carry her across the street, then set her down when we arrived to where Chief Fisher and the woman stood.

"Oh, Travis, hey," the Chief said. "This is Dr. Tina Myers from the National Guard out of Nashville. Dr. Myers, this is Travis Grady."

"You can call me Tina," she extended her hand. "Are you an NVI?"

"I'm sorry an ... NVI?" I asked.

"Non-Vaccinated Individual," she explained.

"I am. Are you?"

"Yes, as is every volunteer here," she said. "Is this your daughter?"

"I'm Daisy," my daughter spoke brightly.

"Well, that's a beautiful name."

Really, I wasn't in the mood for small talk. I wanted to know why they were in town and were they able to help.

I asked, "So do you know about all this?"

"I know from what I see," she replied. "Sadly, no one is an expert."

"Do you know if a person hasn't turned ... Lost, if maybe it won't happen?" I questioned. "I mean, are there people that haven't been affected that were vaccinated?"

"I haven't heard of any cases. Again, I am limited to what I have personally witnessed and read in reports, that's not to say it can't happen."

She must have noticed me looking down to Daisy.

"Is Daisy vaccinated?" she asked.

I nodded. "She is. And she's fine."

"Well, that's great news. I'll share that," she said.

"Dr. Myers, here," Chief Fisher said. "Came to help out with late stages. The ones that can't travel. We're going to try to move as many here to the auditorium as we can."

"And do what?" I asked.

Tina answered. "End of life care. Make them comfortable. We have the means for that."

"And those folks?" I pointed to the ones getting in the truck. "Where are they going?"

"Franklin. We have volunteers there," Tina said. "They will help with the transitioning to end of life. It's difficult. Fortunately, more people are rallying to help than those healthy and taking advantage of things."

"That's happening?" I asked.

"You'd be surprised," she replied. "Or maybe not. Are you a volunteer in town?"

Before I could answer, Chief Fisher did. "Travis has been dealing with his own situation. He lost his boy a couple days ago in a tragic wandering accident. And his wife ...his wife has been hanging on."

"Will you be bringing her here or will she go to the facility in Franklin?" Tina asked.

"My wife will stay home, thank you."

Daisy spoke up. "Mommy doesn't talk anymore. She isn't moving or eating."

There was something about hearing my daughter say those words and the look on the doctor's face when she heard them.

"Mr. Grady, if you want, I can give you some medication or I can come take a look ..."

"No, we're fine," I abruptly stopped her. "In fact, we need to go. Come on Daisy."

"Mr. Grady." She walked to me, stopping us. "It can get very challenging. Please know we're here. If you need anything, please just stop by."

"Thank you but no, I can handle my wife."

I walked off with my daughter. I don't know why I shunned the help or even the medication. Maybe it was another slap of reality or maybe I didn't want to admit I needed help.

Handling my wife was easier said than done. I wanted to handle her, take care of her. What I and others were dealing with was a rapid decline that we were ill prepared for.

It was fast.

I hated myself because it killed me to even look at her.

How did Maranda go from a vibrant and creative woman to a mere shell of everything I loved and adored?

She didn't even look like herself. Her hair suddenly grew dull, her face drawn and pale. She stared out with lifeless eyes and mouth agape. She wasn't gasping for breath, but she looked like she was barely breathing. I propped her up in bed on pillows, and she hadn't moved, laying slightly on her side legs curled and hands drawn in.

It was heartbreaking.

While I wanted to say I couldn't believe she was holding on so long, it didn't surprise me. Maranda was a fighter.

When we arrived back home. Daisy said she was hungry. I was glad to hear that. She barely ate since Beau had died.

The cupboards were pretty bare and I had taken the last of the freezer stuff out the night before. I knew there was food in town, stuff I could get, but I hadn't gone out. I literally was taking us down to nothing.

Pickings were slim and there was some pancake mix left in the box. Enough to make a batch. I guess I was in the flow, focusing on making my daughter a meal when I heard my daughter's scream.

As a parent you can recognize the type of cries and screams, and hers was riddled with fear and pain.

Had she hurt herself?

Stopping immediately what I was doing, I followed the screams. They were high pitched and continuous. They came from the first floor and I found her in my bedroom.

Daisy stood next to the bed, desperately trying to get away, but Maranda clutched on to her arm.

My daughter struggled to get free, crying out while Maranda stared at her, making this noise, this throaty noise. I rushed to the bed and immediately grabbed on to Daisy, but not only was Maranda's grip tight, her fingernails dug into the under part of Daisy's forearm, drawing blood.

I literally had to pry Maranda's fingers from my daughter. When she was free, Maranda began making that noise louder and Daisy grabbed onto me, jumping into my arms.

"I just wanted to see Mommy, I just wanted to see her," Daisy sobbed.

"I'm sorry, I'm so sorry." I cradled her, carrying her from the bedroom.

I took her straight to the kitchen to wipe off her arms, Daisy sobbed the entire way there. Sitting her on the counter, I turned on the sink, trying like hell to block out the moans and cries of

Maranda.

"Why won't she stop?" Daisy asked crying. "Why is she doing that?"

I focused on wiping off her arm. But it was hard to ignore the aching, non-verbal yelling of my wife. It was as if she were trying to say something, calling out for something, but what?

After I finished Daisy's arm, placing bandages on the small fingernail cuts, I lifted her from the counter. "Go to your room and turn the music up really loud. Okay."

She nodded quickly and raced away.

I really didn't understand my thought process at that moment, or why I instructed Daisy to do that. The moment, I heard her footsteps on the stairs, a part of me knew and I walked back to the bedroom, closing the door.

The cries from Maranda were loud, steady and almost rhythmic. They had this off tune, demonic sound to them.

She lay half on her side, the bed and night dress soiled, her arm outstretched as if she still were reaching for Daisy.

Who was this woman on the bed? This mere ghost of the woman I married. I loved her, but the person she was had left us and she who remained was fighting with every last ounce of her strength not to let go.

Or was she?

Maybe the cries were those of pain, frustration … cries for help.

She shifted her eyes, looked at me and screamed out even louder.

I wanted to cover my ears, instead I closed my eyes, wishing it would stop. Just stop. Please stop.

It didn't.

My wife, my beautiful wife didn't deserve what was happening to her. No one that was inflicted deserved it. It was horrendous, heartbreaking and demoralizing.

Gone was her being, her dignity.

If I knew my wife, and I believed I did, she wouldn't want to be like that.

I ... didn't want her to be like that.

But all the wishing in the world wasn't going to make it stop.

And it had to stop.

"I'm sorry, Maranda, sweetie, I am so sorry." I stepped to the bed, leaned down and kissed her on the forehead. "I'm so sorry."

Lifting the pillow next to her, I placed it over her face. At first it was gentle, but then as the screams continued, I put more pressure on that pillow.

One hand.

Both.

The screams muffled, then softened and I pushed harder.

Her cries out were the only fight she gave, and they weakened, slowing down, farther apart, until finally .... silence.

It seemed like forever for it to stop, the entire time I held that pillow to her, I felt the pain in my chest and I fought it, pushed it back, shoved any and all emotions away.

My wife had suffered enough.

There was a lot of internal debate in those immediate seconds after. Why did I do it? For Maranda, Daisy or even my own selfish reasons?

Whatever the reason ... it didn't matter.

It was done.

My wife was gone and I had taken her life.

THIRTEEN – FORGIVEN AND FORGOTTEN

I snapped.

Something in me snapped the second I stepped from the bedroom and closed the door. Suddenly, I was this soup of negative emotions. Rage, fear, and panic swept over me and I just wanted to run.

In fact, I did.

I grabbed our coats and my daughter, got in the truck and drove.

I was breaking, I knew it. To do what I did to Maranda whether it was the humane move or not was spawned, in my opinion, from a dark place in my soul. One that recently went black after I lost Beau.

Only a speck existed, the only light I held on to was Daisy.

How much longer would remain to be seen. When that extinguished, no doubt, I would be like the others, a shell of a person, but in a different way.

"Daddy, why are we leaving?" Daisy asked when I put her in the truck. "Daddy, what about Mommy. Where are we going? Daddy what about my booster seat?"

It took everything I had not to say we were running away and never going back. In fact, that's what I wanted to do. Never look back, never go back, just keep going. The only intention I had on stopping was to get gas.

It was all different. The roads were slushy and the highways untouched. Barely any tire tracks at all, just the ones I assumed were from the military. How clear it was that there was very little life. It was like driving around after a snowfall on Christmas afternoon, no traffic, everyone home.

Finally, I came up with an explanation to my daughter. "We're exploring," I told her. "We need to see if people are sick elsewhere. Because there's no more news."

"That's a good idea. Are we going to Aunt Linda's? We are." She pointed out the window. "We just passed the Sugar Shack."

I hesitated before answering, but in my mind I was thinking it was a plan. One I hadn't thought of. I was so wrapped up in my wife and children, I hadn't thought of my sister.

"Yes," I told her. "We need to go check on Aunt Linda and Uncle Steve."

"Okay." Her reply was simple. I wasn't sure how much she absorbed about all that was going on. She seemed naïve, and that was fine with me. The less she comprehended the better. I didn't want whatever remained of her life marked by more death and sadness.

Instantly after stating we were headed to Sweetwater to see my sister, I started making plans. I desperately wanted to believe that my daughter would not fall victim to the vaccine effect, but it was just a matter of time. Because of her age, she was one of the last in town to get it. They waited until she turned four. Perhaps because she had it so much later than anyone else, maybe I'd get another year.

There was no way to know if it worked that way. We were cut off from all news and information, for all I knew, things could be different elsewhere. To me, that was a possibility. Why else were they taking people from town, three hours away to Franklin?

Again, so focused on Maranda and Beau, we were in a bubble and I now was on the highway out of it.

Not long before arriving at Sweetwater, I spotted the dark cloud in the distance, it hovered on the horizon. It wasn't a storm cloud, it was smoke. Not a lot, but reminiscent of what I had seen in my town.

Something was obviously burning.

It wasn't the town, at least I hoped not. As I came over the slight grade in the last stretch of the highway to Sweetwater, I saw two pickup trucks parked there and two men standing in the road.

It was odd enough to see that, but when they raised their rifles, I immediately hit the brakes, stopping about thirty feet from them. I thought of backing up and speeding away, but then they walked our way.

Why were they doing it? Protecting the town? From what?

"Why do they have guns?" Daisy asked, as they walked to the truck.

"I don't know." I wound down the window. "Everything alright?" I asked of the man who approached my side. I tried not show I was nervous. Not for myself, but my child.

"Hey, there," he replied. "You know your name?"

"Yep. Travis Grady from High Water. I'm here to check on my sister who lives here. Can I get through?"

"Yeah, we're just making sure those driving through aren't … you know, Lost. We have too many come through plowing into buildings, people …"

I nodded. "We've had that, too."

"You're fine?"

"Well, if I wasn't, would I know?" I retorted with a nervous chuckle. "But I am. I was not vaccinated."

"How bad is it in High Water?" he asked.

"Bad."

"Yeah, here too. But, you know how it is, we do what we can to help."

Actually, I didn't. Unlike the man who stood at my window, Chief Fisher and others, I was focused on my own.

"Well, I hope your sister is alright," he said. "She doesn't live near Elm and Stewart does she?"

"No, on North Sixth."

"Good. Good. We had a gas explosion there yesterday."

"Is that the smoke?" I asked,

"That's just a fire. They happen. The explosion flattened an entire block."

"Caused by The Lost?" I asked.

He nodded. "Yep. I heard it's like that in a lot of places. The Lost don't know, leave the stove on ... or turn a valve. One of many freak things that occur. It's been insane here. When you're looking for your sister, just... just know, trains came and took a lot of folks to a facility."

"In Franklin?"

"No, Nashville."

"Ain't that like the same difference?"

"I guess. But Tara Rose is at the Library, she has a list of all that were taken. If your sister isn't home, you can check there."

"Do you have a lot of people not vaccinated, not affected?" I asked. "I know you have almost twice as many people living here."

"Yeah, we have a good bit. A hundred and two registered to volunteer."

"Wow, we have twelve."

"We had no idea, there's been no word from High Water. I'll talk to Council to see if they can send some help."

"Thank you, I appreciate it."

"Good luck."

I put my window back up, gave him a nod of thanks and pulled forward.

I knew already it was different in Sweetwater, and I held high hopes that difference extended to my sister.

Perhaps it was my lack of leaving the apartment that I didn't see the organization in High Water. I couldn't imagine with only twelve people it was anything like Sweetwater.

The main business district of Sweetwater, unlike my town, was a one-sided street. All the buildings were on one side of the road, sandwiched between them and the railroad tracks was a parking lot and a small, half-circle flag park. In between them was an oddly placed gazebo.

When we drove through, that entire area, the parking lot, the flag park and gazebo were tents and trailers. Smoke rose from a winter barbecue grill and people carried plates, eating. They were dressed in winter work gear.

I passed a truck, they were loading bodies. No one looked or glanced our way as we drove by. I made a mental note of the library's location, it was busy, folks going in and out. Sweetwater pulled it together, a part of me was envious, and knew if Daisy and I stayed there, I would probably have no choice but to help as well.

Was it like this everywhere? Or did just the small towns decide they had to be neighborly.

I couldn't imagine a big city like Nashville having the volunteer power. In fact, I imagined the opposites. Opportunist taking advantage of a world falling apart.

I didn't really connect the dots of my sister's house and the gas explosion until I turned at the end of the main street. Three blocks down it was another world.

That gas explosion was far more devastating than I was led to believe or maybe I just didn't register what it had done.

The entire area I drove through was flattened. Buildings and homes reduced to sticks of timber and mounds of bricks. Small amount of smoke hovered over the debris from the smoldering fires.

I felt like I was driving through a different type of apocalypse, one brought on by bombs, maybe even a meteor. The area was just decimated.

Finally, we made our way around it to my sister's street. I always loved her house. It was one of those homes that had a partial second floor. It always seemed too modern for Sweetwater.

Her black SUV was parked out front and the porch light was on.

I pulled into the driveway and waited. I racked my brain trying to remember if she had the vaccination. Did her husband? I couldn't recall and that filled me with optimism. But then, why hadn't she called? Although, since Maranda fell victim, I hadn't called her either.

"Stay here," I told Daisy. "Let me check first okay?"

"Okay, Daddy."

"Don't get out of the truck."

"I won't."

I glanced at my daughter, her little pink knit cap pulled nearly to her eyebrows. I felt confident she wasn't going anywhere. After leaning in and kissing her on the forehead, I got out of the truck and walked to the door.

I rang the bell, waited, then knocked. "Linda," I called out. Sidestepping, I peeked in the living room window and didn't see anything. I was going to attempt to open the window, then I thought about trying the door first.

It wasn't like in the movies where some key was hidden. If it was locked, my only options were trying the back door then a window.

Of course, the front door was locked. I informed Daisy I was going to try the back. Fortunately, the kitchen door was open.

I was frightened of what I'd find. When I stepped in, the house smelled stale and a little moldy.

Dishes were stacked in the sink and a sauce pot was on the stove with remnants of dried up soup.

Walking from the kitchen and into the living room, I knew something wasn't right. It was messy. Papers on the floor, cushions from the couch were disheveled. The pictures on the sofa table were knocked over.

I lifted one to set it straight and saw it was a family reunion picture from a decade earlier. Beau was just a toddler and I held him on my hip.

We all were smiling, wearing shorts. It was hot that day, I remembered, and Beau's hair was curly from the humidity.

There wasn't a sound in the house and fearful my sister had died, I checked every room.

Nothing.

Not a sign. In fact, a couple drawers were open and so was the closet. Had she taken clothes and left?

My next course of action was to go to the library and check there. See if the woman keeping tabs knew anything about my sister.

I couldn't stay much longer and leave Daisy in the truck. Taking that family reunion photo, I walked out the front door. As I made it to the truck, that's when I noticed it across the street. The tricycle. It set in the lawn of the house, on its side. The snow had melted enough to expose it.

A tricycle meant a child.

I hadn't given much thought to that aspect of it all, maybe because it was far too horrific to think about.

What happened to all the children?

Was that even a question I wanted an answer to?

I got back into the truck, placing the photograph on the seat.

"You okay?" I asked Daisy.

She looked at me and slowly nodded.

"Aunt Linda wasn't there. We're going to go into town. Okay?"

I put the truck in gear and proceeded to drive. It would only take a few minutes. I needed to find out if my sister was on that train or worse, did something happen.

I believed that trip to Sweetwater was what I needed. It truly did take my mind off of what happened with Maranda. But that reprieve was short. When I pulled into a spot by the library, my phone rang.

I looked down to the number.

It was Chief Fisher.

A wave of 'first date', 'new job', 'waiting on medical test results' type of nerves rushed over me and before I could answer that call, I saw a flash of Maranda's face, the look in her eyes just before I placed that pillow on her.

I knew that was why the Chief was calling.

Hands shaking, I answered the phone stating, "Hold on, Chief" then I opened the truck door and took the call as I stood outside.

"Travis," he said. "Why did you run?"

I didn't mean to act dumb, it just came out that way. "What do you mean?"

"Travis, we saw you barrel out of town. I went to your place. Travis, I know."

There was something about the way he said that, firm yet unemotional. It stumbled me and my back hit into the driver's door. It took everything I had to keep it together. I could feel it welling in my gut, the breaking factor. I wanted to cry out, to sob.

"Chief, I ...."

"Travis, we know. We understand."

"I killed her. I just ... I killed her," I blurted emotionally.

"I know," he said. "Are you alright?"

"What?"

"Are you alright? Where are you now?"

"Sweetwater. I just panicked, I ran. I was looking for Linda."

"When you get your answers. Come home. No one will judge you. We're gonna move her from the home, Travis. Is that alright?"

I didn't answer.

"Travis."

"Yes," I said. "Yes, I'm sorry."

"I understand. I just wanted to let you know that."

"Thank you."

"See you soon."

I didn't say 'goodbye', I was too emotional. I just hung up. I took a few seconds leaning against my truck to compose myself. I didn't need Daisy to see me upset and I knew, it wouldn't take much to make me crumble.

Once I believed I was composed, I took a deep breath and walked around the front of the truck to get to the passenger door for my daughter.

Only a woman stood there staring at me.

"Are you alright, sir?" she asked. "I saw you out here. Marty said your truck went through."

"Are you Tara?"

"I am. Can I help? I know this must be tough."

"Um, yeah, I was looking for my sister. I went to her house and she wasn't there and I was ...."

"Oh." Her expression of surprise caught my off guard.

"Oh?" I asked.

"I thought, you know, you needed help with your daughter."

At first I thought, 'what a strange statement to make', and then as I questioned with, "My daughter?" I spun around to look into the truck.

Daisy had both her hands flush against the passenger's window, staring blankly out as she repeated tapped her forehead against the window.

There had to be some sort of mistake, or confusion. My five year old was just being odd or quirky. I rushed to the door and opened it.

"Daisy?"

She looked at me and screamed in terror.

"Daisy." I reached for her and she kicked and screamed.

No. No. It wasn't happening.

Not my baby.

That fast.

I flung the door open all the way, undid her belt and despite her struggles, her wails for help, I grabbed her and clutched her.

On the sidewalk, I crumbled, knees buckling to the snow covered concrete with my hysterical daughter in my arms.

I was a stranger to her, she was scared of me. And I, at that second was completely and utterly broken.

It was over.

Nothing good would remain.

Even if I wanted to deny it, the painful truth was ... the last person left that I loved, my baby, was now one of The Lost.

I wasn't strong enough to handle it nor would I ever be.

It was that moment, I knew, one way or another, my life would soon be over.

FOURTEEN – TO THE GROUND

March 18 – Three Weeks Later

"Travis Grady, rise and shine."

I knew that gruff voice. It was the same one that woke me nearly every morning for the previous couple weeks. Finding me, waking me up wherever I passed out.

Joe Randal.

His usually hoarse and rough voice was growing particularly hoarser and rougher by the day.

He was tired.

He didn't stop.

Joe was a good guy. I had known him at least twenty years. He was older than me, about a decade. He wasn't tall or short, just somewhere in between, and he always wore a baseball cap.

Four kids, a wife, two small grandbabies and they were all gone.

Yet, Joe kept going.

I didn't want to hear it at first.

When Daisy died, I was done. Joe came to my home every day. Tried to sober me up. I was the guy who had the occasional beer and suddenly, I was drinking nonstop.

Slobbering, passed out drunk.

Joe would wake me, wash me, get some coffee in me and drag me out.

Even when it was right after I lost Daisy, he had me out.

"You got to keep going," Joe told me.

"I don't want to keep going. I don't want to live."

"Yeah, well, neither do I. Now is not the time to die."

I didn't know what the hell that was supposed to mean.

There was too much work to be done and I didn't see the point.

I knew there were still a few people left that were dying, but they were finding bodies, moving them. A dozen people cleaning up the town. Why?

"We start here and move on. People lived and loved, we can't just leave them to rot where they are," Joe said. "Is that a fair testament to their life? Don't those who built this world deserve more."

He was like this spokesperson, or salesman of the post apocalypse world. If the end game was to get the survivors together, why wouldn't we just go somewhere and start a new life?

Joe used an analogy.

"Say your wife has a girls' night out, first one in a long time. You're home with the kids," Joe explained. "You're playing video games, they got their dolls and action figures, LEGOs everywhere. You're eating junk food, just not caring. Do you pick up as the night goes on or do you save it all for later, only to get too tired and pass out. Your wife comes home to a disaster. It's the same thing. Do we want to leave a mess for those destined to keep on living? I know I don't want future generations coming to High Water, seeing a town a mess with skeletons and stuff. What's that say about us and how we cared for those in this town?"

Admittedly, when he first gave that speech and he gave variations more than once, I didn't care. But once Joe actually got me out of the apartment, I kind of got it.

Work kept me focused, it helped me not to think and I didn't want to go back.

Going back meant reliving memories I didn't want to face.

So, I resorted to doing my part and sleeping where I could. Most of the time, even though the weather was still cold, it was in my truck. But I had on a couple occasions fallen asleep on the park bench not far from the canned bonfire we all gathered around at the end of the night.

That was where Joe found and woke me.

"Stiff?" Joe asked.

"No, not really," I stretched and sat up. "It wasn't too cold last night."

Joe reached down and lifted the empty bottle of vodka. "I'd say you found a way to warm yourself."

"It was almost empty."

Joe grumbled a 'hmm'. "Well, we're all gathering at the diner right now. Get warm, get coffee. Marty and Tara from Sweetwater are here to help."

I grunted a little in disgust.

"What? You don't like them?"

"No, it's the diner. It smells in that section of town."

"That's because there are three hundred bodies in the Municipal Building," Joe said. "The whole town smells, but one place at a time. Buscio's first, then the Municipal Building."

"Instead of taking the bodies out to burn, we should seal them up and wait it out."

"Jesus, Travis. Would you feel that way if your family was still in there?"

I only glanced up to him.

"Must be something in the air, because everyone seems to be hating on the body gathering part."

"Can you blame them?"

Joe simply gave a 'follow me' and walked away.

We headed to the diner, and I hated the wave of smell that hit me. Just before we walked in. In my opinion we weren't making much progress. Sweetwater needed to send more than two people to help out.

At least the diner had a better smell, coffee and something cooking. Everyone looked at me when I walked in, like from one of those movies where everything stops when a stranger enters a small town diner.

It was only a quick glance at me and then they returned to looking at the television. It was on, but only sound and no picture. Just a blue screen.

There weren't many in the diner. Just those who remained from my town. Originally there were twelve of us, but we lost one woman to a heart attack and two others when they took their own lives.

No one could blame them.

Chief Fisher did this fast point of his hand and only whispered, "Coffee." He like the others were listening to the woman on the television.

I half listened as I walked to the coffee pot and poured a cup, then my senses kicked in as I took that first sip.

"... are doing our best to keep the lights on and water running," she said. "We have the volunteer units working hard. These are the same people that came into your cities and towns to help with The Lost. If you lose essential services, please contact us at the number on the screen."

I glanced up, telephone numbers scrolled up like credits.

"Phones are still in service and we intend to keep them that way," she continued. "We also are asking to report any trouble in or around your area. We encourage rural areas to take in those who come your way. I promise we'll have the hubs assigned in the weeks to come. Please be patient. I'll update at four pm. Thank you."

Static.

Chief Fisher raised the remote and aimed it at the television. "At least they're updating now. Something is going. Life is out there."

"She didn't say much," I said.

"You missed a bunch sleeping on that bench out there," Chief Fisher replied.

"What's this hub thing she mentioned."

"Oh ... they're trying to gather the population into certain areas. That's all I know."

"Anything else good?" I asked.

"Not really," he replied. "Out west is pretty bad, she didn't get into details. But suggested that the town have a security team."

I laughed. "We barely have a cleanup team."

"We do what we can," the chief said.

"I get it. I do. But we have eleven hundred homes in this town. We only hit about twenty a day because we take twenty out of Buscio's a day to bury while we cremate twenty."

"You got another suggestion, Travis?" he asked.

"Yep." I nodded. "I think we have surpassed the time to give every person some tender loving care. I mean…" the room erupted with grumbles. "What? We're burying each person individually. That's a lot of work. I mean I liked these folks, too."

"Travis," The Chief said my name sternly. "What are you saying?"

Joe Randal answered. "He thinks we should seal up the buildings and move on?"

Terri turned around and looked at me. "You mean let them just decompose forever?"

"Well, yeah, no sort of," I replied. "It will eventually stop. We get some lime and cover them, then plastic the windows."

Chief Fisher shook his head. "Your family is in the ground Travis, you don't think the others in town deserve the same?"

"That ain't fair, Chief," I said. "Does anyone in this room have family still out there, not buried? No. I'm not saying everybody. I'm saying the ones in the funeral home and Municipal Building. It stinks to high heaven."

"So do you," the Chief said. "But you don't see us wanting to cover you with lime and seal you off somewhere."

"Hey, now, that's not right," I defended.

"So you're saying just pretend the bodies aren't in town?" the chief asked.

"Nope. Not at all," I shook my head. "Just the Municipal Building and funeral home. We can focus on the houses and the people in there."

I expected another round of groans and backlash, but no one

said anything.

"Unfortunately, Travis." The chief walked my way toward the coffee. "Not a single person in this room has the heart to cover their neighbors with lime and let them rot where they are."

The ding of the bell above the diner door drew my attention and Marty from Sweetwater walked in.

"Sorry," he said. "We got held up. We're ready to help."

Then Tara Rose walked in. Marty I had seen a couple times, Tara, it had been since that day in Sweetwater. The day my Daisy turned Lost.

I kinda froze, the memories of seeing her sent a jolt into me.

"How are you doing, Travis?" Tara walked up to me. "Are you okay?"

My mind went immediately to the library that day three weeks earlier.

"Are you okay?" Tara asked.

"No, I'm not." I kept trying to block out Daisy's cries.

My little girl sobbed, so scared. She cried over and over, "I want my mommy. I want my Daddy."

"What do I do?" I asked Tara.

"The guard is still here," Tara said. "You can go with them to Nashville. That's where your sister is. Take her there."

"I can't. I can't. She's all I have left, I just can't take her away."

"Once the mind goes, it's done. There's no coming back," Tara said. "She doesn't know who you are."

It wasn't possible. It was literally a snap of a finger. I heard what she said that day, but I didn't believe it.

"Travis?" Tara called my name.

"I'm sorry," I snapped out of. "I'm ... I'm doing. Not okay. Not bad, just doing."

"That's all of us. Did you ever ... did you ever find your sister?"

I didn't say it, but I thought, 'wow, I hadn't even tried'.

I lowered my head some, shaking. “A little ashamed to say I haven’t.”

“It’s alright.” She grabbed my arm compassionately. “A lot has happened.”

I looked up when the chief called for everyone to come outside for assignments. Something he did every morning. Sending us in pairs. I was certain it was my turn again for the funeral home. I hated it there and I knew if it was bad there, I couldn’t imagine how bad it would be at the Municipal Building when we finally got there.

I started to head outside when my phone rang.

It was an odd ring, and I was surprised it still was charged, it had been a couple days since I plugged it into my car.

I pulled my phone from my pocket as I headed out of the diner and it just looked weird. I didn’t recognize the number, but after a second I realized it was one of those video calls.

Everyone stopped and looked at me.

“Well, answer it Travis,” Joe Randal said with some excitement. “Who is calling you.”

I was certain it had to be some wrong number, then I answered it.

Everyone watched with anticipation. I didn’t see the big deal.

The call connected and it was Doctor Jon Yee. He looked like he was walking and he kept looking back over his shoulder.

“Whoa,” I said. “Hey, Doctor Yee.”

“Jon, call me Jon, Travis. I know it’s probably strange for me to call you.”

“Well, yeah, everyone is watching. They’re kinda shocked my phone rang.”

“Travis, you’re the only person I knew without a doubt wasn’t getting this thing. I need ... how are things in your small town?”

“Not good. Not many of us left,” I told him. “We’re cleaning up. It smells pretty bad around here.”

“You’re not looking like you smell too good yourself.”

"Yep, well, that's the general consensus."

"But are things okay there?" he asked. "Are those of you who are left, are you staying there?"

"I guess so. There's this hub thing, but not sure what we're doing about it. Why?"

"I need some place to go. I want to go where I at least know someone. Things are bad out this way. They are."

"What do you mean bad?" I questioned.

"Looting, madness. Just total chaos. I can't get food. Gangs have just taken over."

"It's not that way here."

"Then you're lucky. I'll see you soon. I'm on my way."

"You're gonna drive all the way across the country just to get to High Water? Are things that bad out there?"

"Yeah, and I'm willing to bet they're bad out that way, too. You're just lucky. See you soon my new friend."

The call made a beep as it disconnected. He was a stranger, someone I met over a free drink at Reilly's, waiting on wings and George's unfortunate and tragic accident.

Now he was rushing twelve hundred miles? That call made me realize I had watched life end through a view with my small town goggles, but I didn't have a real clue about what was happening to the rest of the world.

Maybe, eventually, I needed to take a look.

What else did I have to do?

<><><><>

Buscio's was a catalyst to a lot of things I did that day. I knew I'd be teamed up with Joe and he and I would be on Funeral Home duty. The Chief tended to make everyone go once a week and no work on Sundays. I didn't get what was up with that. Then again, a surviving High Water resident was the pastor.

Everyone went to church, ate a meal. To Hell with the smell. No matter where you lived in town you smelt it.

It was worse near the funeral home and Municipal Building.

Joe asked me not to bitch all morning about how bad it was.

I didn't think I needed to bitch.

It was evident on Joe's face when we walked into the funeral home. It all but screamed that he knew something had to be done.

What could be done? Not only did we have very few people, everyone operated on a Sunday mentality. Instead of being Sunday drivers, they were Sunday body movers. I could only move as fast as the person I was with. And at the funeral home, no matter how fast we wanted to get bodies out of there, it wasn't going to happen.

They were still packed in there like sardines, stacked on top of each other. The recent arrival of spring like weather sped up the decay process. Not only did it smell, it was just gross.

Bodies were rotten, spoiled to the point it was the worse smell ever. I even had dryer sheets in my mask and it didn't do all that well, they were the good sheets too.

When we brought in Beau, it was the early stages of it all. When folks weren't dying left and right. Bodies were covered, placed nearly everywhere. But as time went on it was evident, they were just tossed there with the decision to worry about it later.

Moving them wasn't easy. They were breaking down, like rotting potatoes, leaving a sticky film and the ones that were layered were glued with the bodily substances.

We could fit a bit more than twenty bodies into the truck, but it was hard loading them. Not like in movies where they showed people tossing the dead. That wasn't the case. Twenty seemed to be the limit and we still had to take them out to the empty field off the highway where Skeeter had dug a hole with the back hoe.

It was emotionally tough, too. It wasn't a matter of 'they're just bodies' they were neighbors, friends. People you saw at the store, kids that went to school with your own.

It was gut wrenching and after a long morning, a break was

needed.

I was just as guilty for not doing more.

It was too damned hard.

Again, I knew there was a faster way. When we took the mid-afternoon break and all gathered at the diner for soup, I knew from looking at the faces how exhausted everyone was, it was time to bring it up again.

"Soup?" Chief Fisher asked. He was serving himself a cup.

"No thanks."

"We're rationing," he said. "You sure?"

"Why are we rationing," I asked. "Seriously."

"Because it's going to be a while until things stockpile, if they ever do," he replied. "If we don't join up with another group or bigger group, we may be forced to grow our own. Until then we ration what's in town."

"Eleven hundred and two homes, a grocery store, and we ration?"

"It's not that much," he replied. "Not for long term."

"Heck, then we hit the Costco," I said. "They actually have a huge distribution center in Franklin, it's new, unless that's where they put our people."

"You know, for a man who wouldn't leave his house, lift a finger, you sure are full of ideas in the aftermath. You sure you don't wanna just take over?" Chief Fisher said with some sarcasm.

"I'm just making suggestions about food."

"You gonna go make runs there?" Chief Fisher asked.

"Sure, why not."

"Then go ahead. Good luck to you. I wouldn't."

I had no idea why he said that or what he meant by that. It was a warehouse with food, what was the problem?

I was going to ask him to elaborate, when I noticed Terri.

Terri looked especially bad, she lifted the spoon in her soup, letting the liquid fall back down.

"I'm not gonna ask if you're okay," I told her, "I can see you're not. Can I do anything?"

"No." She shook her head. "It was just bad today. How did we forget Travis?" she asked. "We're the ones that were supposed to remember."

Joe stepped into the conversation. "We didn't forget, we just didn't think. Too much going on."

"The Gillian Family was a lot to handle," Pastor Monroe said and looked at me. "They had that newborn and we just ..."

"Stop." I lifted my hand. "I can't hear that, if I do, all I'll do is think about the babies we didn't help or save. I just ..." I stepped out to the center of the diner. "Why are we doing this to ourselves?

Pastor Monroe asked. "What do you mean? What are you talking about?"

"For three weeks, longer for you guys, every single day we go out, we search for the dead, we take them out, we bury them, we pray for them. It's too much. For all of us. This isn't helping us move on. That's if we want to move on. It needs to end. I know I don't want to go back into Buscio's and face that. It was bad today, I don't want to think about how bad it will be next week. These are no longer our friends and neighbors, they're just bodies."

"That's terrible," Pastor Monroe said.

"Is it?" I asked. "You're not tired, Pastor? You're not tired of the bodies? Not tired of going out every day doing the same thing."

"No," he replied strong. "Because that is all I have to do. When that's done, then what? Sit around thinking?"

"Planning," I said. "Plan for the future."

"Is that really what you want, Travis?" The pastor asked. "You really want to think about the future?"

"Nope. But I think it's a hell of a lot easier than thinking about the now. And the 'now' is not where I want to be."

"Sadly," Chief Fisher interjected. "You can't get to the future without facing the now."

"So let's make the now go a bit faster then."

Chief Fisher shook his head slightly confused. "What are you talking about?"

"Just what I said. We make it go faster."

Joe Randal shook his head. "There's no way to make it go faster. There just isn't. This isn't some bank account you screwed up so you open a new one. Or the post office that got so far behind they ditched and burned ten thousand pieces of mail. There's no quick clean here."

"Travis, son, we are moving and doing the best we can," the Chief said. "One day at a time, one body at a time. We'll get there. There are only a handful of us. Other than leave town or burn it down, there's no quick erase. We just keep going."

I heard what I would call a proverbial bell, but it wasn't the one above the door.

I had been helping them for three weeks and we hadn't made a dent. I couldn't speak for anyone else, but every day and every body drilled another hole into my sanity.

At that moment, I truly did snap. All the days that the Chief beat on my door and my head about helping, guilting me to be a 'team player' a 'good neighbor', help out.

It was useless.

It was going nowhere nor would it. They had no end game.

None.

Their lives consisted of just picking up pieces and doing it slowly so they never had to finish and face the reality of what life would have to offer.

I got it. I did. I didn't want to face it either, but there was no real choice.

I was losing it, I couldn't image how the others weren't. As cold as it sounded, it had to be done faster and like I suggested, there was one way to do it.

If they wouldn't.

I would.

By no means would anyone consider me a go-getter. All my life, I went with the flow. About the only thing I went and got was that building we bought; and it took years to get it where me and Maranda wanted it to be.

Parts of that place were still not finished nor would they ever be.

There was one thing I was certain of.

I was dying inside.

How I was still walking, talking, even functioning was beyond me. I had lost everything. Every ... single ... thing. In all honestly, I just wanted to die. But that tiny part of me that doubted if there was really an afterlife, a heaven, was the only thing that kept me from slicing my wrists.

If there was no heaven, then it would all be for naught. I wouldn't be reunited with my family, the only thing that it would accomplish would end the pain I felt with every breath, every day.

A pain I felt I deserved because I lived.

There was something I could do to stop the madness I thought was happening in High Water. The insanity of the dead routine.

Every day. Get up, get coffee, grab a cracker, get assignments and get bodies. Any houses had to be marked.

After that, lunch, then bury the dead.

Same thing.

Go to sleep, get up and do it again.

We were all turning into emotional zombies.

It defined insanity. Doing the same thing over and over again expecting a different result, except there was none.

We weren't even scavenging the homes.

What exactly was the use?

For those who wanted to move on, to try to find peace, that daily reminder routine of how many died had to end.

At least for me.

If I ended it? Or at least a good part of it, what would they do? Kick me out of town?

Did I have the right to do so?

At that point, I didn't really care.

Enough was enough.

Never in a million years did I think that I would take such an initiative.

I was always told grief had five stages. When my father passed suddenly, I remember Pastor Monroe himself telling me, 'There is no set stage to the cycles you'll go through or how long each one will last, or even how fast you'll change. You just have to go with it."

The stages denial, anger, bartering, depression, and acceptance.

Not necessarily in that order and certainly not at all applicable with the ARC Vaccine effect.

There was no denying it and there would never be any acceptance.

Just depression and anger.

I had understandably been stalled in the depression stage for so long that I didn't recognize how welcome that anger phase felt until I walked out of the diner, filled with a sudden rage

Do it, Travis, do it.

Did that anger come from nowhere? Absolutely not. I hated life, I hated myself and I had nothing left.

The survivors in High Water were good people. They were literally in a dead rut, hamsters in a wheel, round and round they went, and I stepped off.

I didn't want to think too much about it because if I did, I wouldn't go through with it.

In my mind, in my distorted reasoning, if we broke the routine, stopped lifting rotting bodies that in some way, we'd start to heal or die if that was the path chosen.

Knowing what I had to do, I went immediately to the print shop.

It dawned on me that I hadn't been there since that day I went for wings. I called in once to take time off when Maranda took ill and that was it.

I pulled the truck to the loading dock, unlocked and raised the door.

Of all the places in town, I wasn't expecting the smell of death to be there. I didn't go searching the cause of the odor, someone in a wayward state went to work and never left. I passed my office, the little room with a window that looked out onto the floor and I paused. My light was still on, my desk was a mess, just the way I always left it, but one thing stood out.

The picture of Daisy.

There were other pictures on my desk, but the back of those frames faced me. Daisy's picture was staring right at me. It was her kindergarten picture. I walked into my office and lifted it. Her eyes were so bright and that smile big, forced and cheesy. It broke my heart to look at it.

She was my baby and, in that picture, she was so full of life.

The spark on her face was lost before I lost her.

Daisy's death was different than Maranda's and Beau's.

Beau's was fast, unexpected and crushing. My head spun, I couldn't figure out what to do next, but I had Maranda and Daisy to grab on to.

Maranda's bout with The Lost went on far too long, it was hard and slow, an undeserving torture as if she had done something so horrible in life that she was getting a payback or purgatory.

But Daisy, she was all I had left. She suffered only three days. Long enough to be too much for her, but not enough for me to process I was going to lose her.

That first day she was combative and angry, she was scared of me as some stranger that kept trying to hug her, and tell her that I loved her. She forgot who she was, who I was.

The second day she stopped talking, she didn't recognize me or react. She forgot how to eat and walk.

The third day... she forgot how to breathe.

I placed the picture down and focused on why I was there. While I didn't know how much to get, I knew what to get, what do use. The print shop had everything I needed. Paper, flammable liquid, combustibles.

After loading my truck, I headed back to town, but first detouring to Reilly's.

It was my own personal liquor store over the previous weeks, seeing how the Chief monitored what we took in town. Everyone forgot about Reilly's.

Although I was hitting that stash pretty good, behind the bar was far from empty and I knew George kept some boxes in the basement.

Carrying that whiskey like it was my own bottle of soda or beer, I went to my truck and sat for a good hour and a half, drinking whiskey and listening to Garth Brooks.

It got a little fuzzy when I went back to town.

They were all sitting around that campsite set up by the church, I waved as I passed, slowing down enough to do a head count, they were all there. No one would be at either of my destinations.

I said I didn't want to go back to Buscio's but I did. I was numb enough from the alcohol to acknowledge the smell and ignore it in the same breath.

Funny how the one place we didn't load bodies was the basement and that was where I went. Buscio's was a huge wooden building, at least a hundred years old.

I carried my boxes in through the receiving doors, and near the stairs, I placed the compressed ink canister on the stairs, saturated a trail of papers with printer press fluid and before I walked out, I lit them.

I wasn't sure it would even work. I never saw how flammable the ink of press fluid was, I heard about it. There once was a huge fire in China at a printing press and Connor used that story as a warning.

Yet, I witnessed it first hand, those papers lit up leaving a blazing trail to the canister on the stairs.

I left.

Both the funeral home and Municipal Buildings were far enough removed that the flames wouldn't spread elsewhere in town, I hoped.

Of course, I wasn't really thinking clearly.

My plan was, by the time they realized the funeral home was on fire, I would be done with the Municipal Building.

However, I ran into a slight problem.

I had carried the remainder of supplies into the Municipal Building, through the back door and got that started right away. One too many canisters I suppose, because I barely got in my truck when the huge boom of the explosion rang out.

Standing at my open truck door, I watched the flames shoot high from the Municipal Building. As demented as it was, I choked on a laugh. It was crazy, yet seeing that gave me a sense of relief.

I reached in the truck, grabbed my bottle from my seat, and took a swig as I watched the fire for a few seconds.

The moment I saw everyone run down the street, I waved then got back in the truck.

I drove off.

Unlike when I took Maranda's life, I wasn't running away in a panic, or confusion, my mind was clear. I was driving to just drive.

Unsure how long I'd be gone, if I was going for an hour or a month. I knew it was time to find out what was happening beyond the confines of Sweetwater and High Water.

Down an open highway, slightly inebriated, cold spring wind whipping in the open window and Garth Brooks playing, I made my way to Nashville. It was as good a destination as any.

FIFTEEN – HEADS UP

My father played guitar. Whenever I thought of him, he was always holding that guitar. Either it was in his hands playing practice riffs or slung over his shoulder. It was an extension of his body. I'm sure he had ambitions to be a great country star or something like that. I envied his talents. I envied how, even though he worked a full time job fixing cars, he was able to follow his passion every weekend and play in his band.

Sometimes my mother would go, sometimes she wouldn't.

I wanted badly to follow in his footsteps, play the guitar and sing like him. But I didn't have the patience, the talent or the finger strength, so I just absorbed what he did.

Needless to say, music was a big part of our upbringing. No song was too old or too new.

Music was music.

I listened to it all the time and so did Daisy.

When my sister was a little girl, my dad used to sing this old Wayne Newton song to her, "Daddy don't you walk so fast,"

For some reason, Linda hated it. She would yell out, "Stop!" and my dad would laugh.

I never found a song that my Daisy hated, she just loved music.

"Daddy, sing with me. Daddy dance with me," she'd say and I'd oblige if I could.

She wasn't a fan of Garth Brooks though, which baffled me because who didn't like Garth? Daisy was still young though and I figured she'd love him when she got older, like I ended up loving Conway Twitty and Glen Campbell. Artists before my time, like Garth was before hers.

Daisy's time to appreciate the music would never come. Maybe that was why I listened to Garth, it wasn't something my daughter listened to so therefore I didn't have memories.

When I drank, I thought, I wallowed in the thoughts to the point they made me crazy, so I drank some more.

Eventually I'd stop drinking or die from it, one of them would happen.

Driving while drinking was pushing my luck. Russian Roulette behind the wheel of a truck.

Torching the buildings in High Water didn't just reset the dead body count, it reset my drunk and had a weird sobering effect on me. I stopped for gas, grabbed a six pack and continued on.

Of course, I was glad I wasn't trashed, getting gas meant authorizing the pumps, and it gave me a chance to see the smoke rising in the distance from my town. It wasn't an abundance, but enough to let me know things were burning.

My phone still worked, and no one called.

Not sure why I was expecting the Chief to call and blast me.

He didn't.

It didn't dawn on me that something went wrong, that maybe I caused more problems than I anticipated.

None of that crossed my mind, I was far too deep in a selfish, self-destructive mode.

The drive to Nashville was nearly three hours. The second round of drinking started hitting me just as I neared my exit ramp to the Costco distribution warehouse.

It was as I approached the exit, I caught a glimpse of the top of the skyline of downtown Nashville. Daylight was waning and the city just was so dark. It gave that 'black out' feel. Still and quiet.

Not a car on the highway, no one to be seen.

Ninety-nine point five percent of my town's population had died from the ARC reaction. Ninety-eight percent of Sweetwater. Still, Nashville was big. Even with one percent surviving there had to be a light, a car. Yet, nothing.

I had been to the distribution center when it first opened, it had been a good year and I had to rely on a foggy, alcohol induced memory to get there. But my memory, even intoxicated was flawless.

That distribution warehouse was imbedded.

The one and only time I was there was when I applied for a job and had to interview. The print shop that I had worked for looked like it was going under. Business was dying. Conner told us to start looking.

I did. I got the job, but then in a strange irony, our print shop got the bid for the Costco mailers and that saved the business.

There I was again, headed to the distribution warehouse because things were bad in High Water. I wasn't convinced we needed to ration like we did.

Going to people's homes and taking their food seemed almost sacrilegious to Chief Fisher, he acted highly offended whenever I mentioned it.

Costco would suffice. Heck, I probably could live in that warehouse.

It was located off the exit, a mile down the road. It had its own road that led to a fenced in perimeter.

The gate was closed but unlocked.

I stumbled out and opened it, then drove through the large employee parking lot.

There was power in that part of the city, at least at the distribution center. With the sun setting, the parking lot lights were in that 'warm up' phase of amber.

There were trucks around one of the buildings, some even backed up to the loading docks of the building.

Until I figured out what I was getting or even what I was doing, I pulled right up front.

Of the three buildings, the center one had an extension, a small reception area, with glass double doors. I assumed they'd be locked, that I'd have to break in, but I didn't.

The light was on above the entrance, but inside the lobby was dark. However, at the end of the lobby area, directly in front of me, I could see light peeking through the tiny windows of the interior double doors.

There was no smell of death and I welcomed that. It didn't even smell musty.

As soon as I pushed open the set of doors, I stepped into a larger room just before the warehouse portion.

There were boxes in that room, a few with the flaps open, not any in a particular order. When I looked in the first box, I knew someone had packed them to stock up. They probably went to the center and left the boxes forgetting why they came. When it happened, half of the people I knew had a slow start the other half went over in a snap of a finger, leaving things undone, still cooking, then wandering off.

I took a peek inside the boxes. They were filled with all sorts of items. Canned meat, snacks, ramen noodles. I counted seven boxes. I was on the fence about returning to High Water, still maybe I'd leave, but taking that food to town would be a good gesture. It wouldn't make up for burning things, but it would show I cared.

Then again, the Chief could say to me, "Take those boxes of food you thieving, arsonist and shove them up your ass."

It wouldn't hurt to try. Maybe just leave the boxes and go.

I carried them all to the truck, loaded them in and secured them with bungie cords, all while sipping on those beers not thinking of the effects. After I was done, I could have driven back the three hour trip, instead I decided to completely sober up before taking a dark highway.

Two sheets to the wind and a belly full of whiskey and beer, my head was spinning a bit and my eyesight blurry.

Just for a couple hours, that was all I needed. I got back in my truck, turned on the music, cranked up the heat, then closed my eyes and rested my head against the back of my seat.

It was short lived.

Listening to Garth wasn't as much of a salvation or safety net from memories as I thought, he was, until that last song.

The Dance

Usually, I listened but didn't really hear what was being sung. Never did I pay attention to that song.

There were several types of drunks. Angry, happy, flirty, emotional. I was never any of the good ones.

Hearing the words to that song just snapped me from the cab of the truck to my home, the last time I was there.

My last moments with Daisy.

My last dance.

The Dance.

I had done everything I could. Everything that would make my final days with Daisy everything we both needed. Even if she didn't know.

I dropped the ball with Maranda, was blindsided with Beau, but with Daisy, I had a chance. I knew what was coming.

She wore her favorite pajamas, we stayed in her room because that was her favorite place on earth. Pink and purple designs on the wall, white bedroom furniture with typical little girl curtains and bedspreads. Wall to wall stuffed animals and dolls all with a name. Names she gave them.

I played her music constantly. Fed her, wiped her down, kept her perfect and I kept her in my arms. I wasn't letting go until I absolutely had to.

She transitioned fast, too fast. That last day, her tiny mouth stayed agape as she gasped for air every few seconds because she stopped breathing, eyes wide and barely blinking.

I knew ... I knew it was coming. The pauses between the breaths were longer.

In all terminal illnesses and brain deterioration cases, right before the end the dying often experience a lucid moment.

You think, 'wow, they're getting better' but they aren't.

No one in town ever mentioned the 'lucid' moments, they didn't happen with the ARC reaction.

Beau never really got too far into his sickness, and Maranda she moved slowly through every stage with an illness that was savoring every moment, and at the end, she cried out, screaming as if she was fighting a physical manifestation of death and it grabbed her dragging her, trying to take her, but Maranda wouldn't let go.

Daisy was leaving me quietly.

I held her in my arms, music playing, and knowing her favorite thing to do was dance, I slowly swayed, dancing with my daughter. It was the dance that would encompass it all, her first prom, the father and daughter dance I would never get at her wedding, a life she would never have.

She grew weaker in my arms, my cheek to her head, my chest feeling the fading breaths.

But in all that pain, all that sadness, my tiny baby girl gave me a gift.

I felt the grip of her frail fingers against my shoulder. Hands that hadn't moved all day and were lifeless, held on to me. I thought it was my imagination and believed it was until she lifted her head and weakly said, "Daddy."

I got that moment. She knew me, she knew I had her and then she left.

For one brief moment, in her own way, my daughter came back to say goodbye.

I don't believe I cried when she passed, not right then. It was peaceful and shocking at the same time. I was still in the absorption of the moment.

Even though I knew my little girl was gone, I just kept dancing with her.

In the cab of my truck, that final moment played like a movie in my mind. Every detail, even the scent of the lilac soap I used to wash her that last day.

I just wanted to pass out, get away from the torment of the memories of my losses. It hurt far too much. Eventually, I would fall asleep, like I did every other night. Tired, intoxicated and a broken man.

SIXTEEN – ROLL ME OVER

It's a rarity to dream of events that had happened and dream of them exactly how they occurred. The mind has a way of filling in blanks and creating better or worse parts, mostly including something ridiculous, like running around naked.

Usually though, it's our subconscious dumping the true feelings or fears out.

I did some research once about how outside sounds and smells can make their way into and part of your dream. Your body is dead to the world outside, and the noise or smell isn't strong enough to wake you.

That research was after I had the weirdest dream where I was having dinner with my father-in-law and he sounded exactly like the character Peter Griffin, all the while in the dream Maranda just laughed and laughed. Here I fell asleep on the couch while Maranda watched Family Guy.

I never forgot that.

Peter Griffin in my dream didn't make sense until I woke. Just like the dream I had when I passed out in my truck outside the Costco Distribution.

None of it made sense, of course, at the time I didn't even know I was dreaming.

The fires at the Municipal Building and funeral home were the catalysts without a doubt. In the dream I was grilling hot dogs with Joe Randal. He said it was burning, he could smell it.

"That's because I lit the buildings on fire," I told him. *"Maybe it*

wasn't right, but heck, here we are having a barbecue."

Oddly, the Chief and Pastor started yelling something in the background.

"Well, where the hell did they go?" Fisher shouted.

"I don't know. Maybe they were sick," Pastor Monroe replied.

"Both of them?"

I waved my hand. "We're right here. Me and Joe."

They didn't seem to care.

"Fucking asshole," the Pastor said.

"Whoa now, Pastor that is some awfully strong language coming from a man of the cloth," I said.

Chief Fisher shook his head with this angry look marching toward me. "All part of that Franklin group. Bet this asshole is and was too drunk so they left him."

"I'm not drunk," I said. "I'm grilling hotdogs."

Then they both just grabbed for me, rough too and they threw me. It felt real.

It was real.

I realized that when I woke up seconds before slamming to the concrete.

I rolled onto my side, several pairs of legs surrounding me, I lifted my head and I saw the boot coming. It came at me fast and hard, nailing me in the jaw and spinning me on to my back.

A man's voice yelled out, "Get him up!", the same voice that came from Pastor Monroe in my dream.

Peter Griffin syndrome.

Hands grabbed onto me yanking me to my feet by two men. They held me firm, locked onto and under my arms. I couldn't move. I was being humanly strung up to face something.

Everything was slightly blurry and I was in this strange daze, if it wasn't for the pain I would have doubted it was real. I could see the outlines of people, a large group, they were shadows with the outdoor distribution spotlights behind them.

Men and women.

A larger man stepped toward me. He was taller than me,

bulkier, too. An older guy maybe fifty, but intimidating. There was no doubt he was rough, he looked it. He stepped to me, then swung out, nailing me in the same spot I took the boot.

My knees buckled and head dropped.

I wasn't awake enough, or emotionally ready to deal with that.

When he struck me, I heard a woman yell out, "Ray! No."

Head down, I saw my baseball cap on the ground, and this 'Ray' guy, I guessed that was his name, grabbed my hair and lifted my head. His fingers gripped the front of my hair as a means to hold up my head. I could feel the skin pulling on my forehead.

"Who you with?" he asked. His face close to mine. I could smell his odd, sewer breath coming from him, it made me cringe.

"No… no one."

Whap!

"Ray!"

"You with Ryan and Phelps?" he asked. "Huh? Sell them out, they left you."

"Who?"

"Don't play stupid."

"I'm alone. I came … alone."

"To steal our food."

"Your food?" I asked. "It's Costco, how is it yours?"

It was a sincere question, not one meant to be sarcastic, but I guess it came off that way and he didn't like it.

"Fucking thief," he said, then Ray hit me again, this time square in the nose. He followed it with a gut punch and I dropped to the ground again.

My God, it wasn't happening, was it? It was nothing less than a lynching.

I was not a fighter. I had been in two scuffles my entire life and both times it was a draw, I held my own. But I was a teenager. As a grown man, I wasn't going to survive what I knew was coming.

There wasn't time to even try to defend myself. The kicks came hard and fast, one after another. My back, legs, hip and head. Nowhere was safe.

I tried to block them, lifting my arms defensively, attempting to get up, only to be knocked back down.

"Ray!" the woman screamed. "Stop it. You're killing him."

"Get back."

"We got our stuff back Ray," she cried out. "Stop it."

Then they did.

The hard tip of the boot or shoe pushed into my shoulder, rolling me on my back.

I tried to open my eyes, they burned and were heavy. Even blurry, I saw Ray crouch down above me.

"Tell your people, this is their warning. Stay away from our stuff." He stood. "Next time we won't be so nice."

Nice? I thought, then saw it. The bottom of his shoe as it came barreling down.

I was certain he slammed into me, but I didn't feel it. At least I don't remember feeling the pain of that hit. That shoe was the last thing I remembered because it was lights out.

Black.

No dreaming.

No pain.

Out.

I came to feeling the cold air on my face, the sound of an engine, and the sharp pain in my ribs and back aggravated by the vibration of the moving vehicle.

I opened my eyes to see the clear dark skies, the multitudes of stars above me. Looking to my left and right, no one was around, I was alone in the back of a truck.

Every part of my body hurt, and I couldn't move. Even when we stopped, I couldn't sit up. That didn't mean I didn't try, I did. If it was possible to have gained fifty pounds instantly, I did. At least it felt that way.

A squeak of the opening tailgate rang out. My ankles were grabbed and whoever it was pulled me some, not much.

The bed of the truck shook some, with the clomping of feet. He climbed. I thought it was one man until I looked up and saw two.

One at my head, the other at my side.

They didn't say anything, and before I could ask what was going on. They not only lifted me, they threw me out of the truck.

I didn't know what part of me landed first, I swore I bounced to my stomach when I struck the pavement.

Belly down, I lifted my head to see the taillights of the truck.

My truck.

I lowered my head back to the ground, I figured they were going to run me down. I waited for it, prepared for it.

Finish it. End this.

But they didn't.

They did a fast squealing U-turn and sped away.

It was dark, the moon gave some light, but not enough for me to see anything.

I could feel the pebbles of the black top under my hands and face. The cool road felt soothing on my beaten body.

I managed to roll onto my back, and when I did, I heard the crinkling sound. My hand reached for my chest and that was when I felt the paper there. I gripped it and pulled it from me. It was a full sheet and I raised it to my eye level.

It was a note, but it was too dark for me to read and my eyesight was far to blurry to even try.

I didn't know where I was. On a back road or highway.

One thing I did know, I was somewhere they wanted me found.

SEVENTEEN – WANDER

I had rolled into Nashville shortly after five PM, and passed out in my truck sometime after eight. I remembered seeing the clock in the truck when I turned off the music. How long I was out before I took my beating I didn't know, nor did I know how long I was passed out on the road. Long enough to get some strength back, but not long enough for it to be daylight.

There were no sounds, no birds and I managed to stand, not well, but I did.

I was stiff as well as in pain, I couldn't breathe through my nose and my jaw barely opened.

I was definitely on a highway with no signs or anything as far as I could see.

My sense of direction was lost. I had no idea where the truck came from, which way was home or even if I would survive to make it home.

If my recent experiences were a country song it would have been called, 'The Tragic Life of Travis Grady'. But I wouldn't be the only one that song was about.

I was one of many suffering every pain imaginable. Although I was sure my encounter with the Nashville country boy version of a Mad Max gang was pretty unique.

I wasn't feeling sorry for myself, I just felt incompetent.

So I just started walking, not very good and not very fast. A pathetic limp that took everything I had to move a few feet.

Then I felt it. At first, I thought I had some large hematoma on my thigh until I realized it was my phone in my pocket.

Because I worked in that print shop and had a young child, when I got my phone I paid a lot of money for one of those cases that were supposedly destruction proof.

How it was even still in my pocket was beyond me, and if it survived I would be surprised. It hurt to slip my hand into my pocket. Using only the very tips of my fingers I slid it out.

I was thrown to the ground, kicked the crap out of and tossed from a truck, and my phone still lit up. There was a crack on the screen, but it still worked. Almost out of battery and with barely a signal, I thought about sending a message asking for help. Then I wondered who I would call. What would I say? I didn't know where I was and did I even have the right to ask the chief or anyone to help me?

No.

After seeing it was only three in the morning, I activated the low power feature and continued my staggering walk.

I didn't make it far, each step felt like it had to be my last. Cold, weak and shivering, I was pushing it to go even further. My legs were like jelly, wobbling and unstable.

Just when I was ready to collapse, find a place to roll over and die through hypothermia, I saw it not far ahead in the distance. It looked like a car on the side of the road. I could see the back end of it.

Of course, it was dark and it could have been my imagination. But it fueled me enough to keep moving. Sure enough, it was real.

An abandoned car on the side of the road.

The driver's door was wide open and there weren't any interior lights on, which meant that car long had since died.

It was one of those big older cars like my Uncle Ralph had. He was proud of his old New Yorker with the turbo jet engine, crushed velour fabric seats and box body that was built like a tank. A gas guzzling machine from an era gone by. The car was probably driven by a senior citizen like my Uncle Ralph, who sadly, like so many others, pulled over in confusion and just abandoned the car.

At the point I made it to the car, I was all but dragging my right leg like some sort of zombie. I could see as I approached the vehicle from behind that no one was in it, nor did I expect there to me.

I wouldn't be able to drive it, but it would be shelter for the night. A safe place to rest, get out of the cold and be out of sight.

After shutting the driver's door, I opened up the back. Sure enough, like with Uncle Ralph's car, there was a big soft back seat. To me, as exhausted and bad as I felt, it was a bed in a luxury hotel. I slid inside, closed the door, and before I collapsed over, my foot caught it on the floor.

I reached down, it was cloth and I lifted it.

In the dark it was hard to tell, but I thought it was one of those old seat covers. That didn't matter, it was a blanket of sorts. In one motion I brought it over my body as I just dropped sideways onto the seat.

Having been outside for so long, beaten and cold, it felt warm in that car. I was tired, emotionally spent and physically beaten.

I wasn't sure that I would even live through the night, but I was certain I would fall asleep.

And I did. I was out the moment I closed my eyes.

EIGHTEEN – LOST AND FOUND

March 28

It was bright, and I fluttered my eyelids a few times before opening them. For some reason I expected them to hurt or be heavy and swollen. I could feel they were, however not as bad as I thought.

It was warm, that seat cover did the trick, but when I finally opened my eyes, the brightness around me blinded more and it took a second to adjust.

With a 'huh' of confusion, I tried to sit up.

Why wasn't I in the car? Where was I?

A man about my age, maybe a little younger, rushed over to me. A thin guy, he wore a baseball cap and a blue Family Guy tee shirt. Which made me think it was a dream. "Whoa, easy there Buttercup," he said with a really thick southern drawl. "You can't be jumping out of bed."

I rested back and my head sunk into a pillow. I looked around, the room was bright, a blue night stand was next to me, behind that a folded room divider which was also blue.

"Bed? How did I get into a bed?"

"Whoa, wow, this is awesome." He pulled up a chair.

"What is?"

"You're talking. Well, normal like, like you understand what's going on."

"I think I do. I'm confused at how I got here."

He raised his hand. "That would be me. Pete. I brought you. I come in a couple times a day to check on you. How are you feeling?"

"My head hurts. Not as bad as I thought it would. My body aches some. My throat hurts. Weird," I cleared it and tried to swallow.

"You need water." Pete reached for the cup on the night stand. He aimed the straw toward my mouth, and I sipped slowly as he talked. "Your throat hurts because they removed the vent yesterday. They didn't want you on it too long. I remember my pap was on one too long..."

I nearly choked. "A vent. You mean ventilator?"

Pete nodded. "More?" he asked in reference to the water.

I took one more drink then indicated I was done. "Ventilator?" I asked.

"Well, yeah, you were pretty bad there. Ribs broken, lungs filled up. Whole bunch of stuff. That skull of yours was cracked too. Not sure how you lived."

I finally came to enough to take in my surroundings other than it being blue. Glancing down my hand was in a cast, I had an IV going into my other arm.

"How long was I out?" I asked.

"You mean how long were out or how long have you been here?" Pete questioned.

"Is there a difference?"

"Yes, sort of. You were out, like coma out for four days, then you been waking up and fighting the vent, but you were out of it. You'd get sedated. All and all it's been ten days."

"Ten days?" I asked shocked.

"You were pretty bad, bud."

"I feel pretty good for being in a coma. I mean I'm hurting but, I would think I'd be feeling bad. Then again, I haven't gotten up."

Pete shrugged. "Technically though you were in the coma like state a couple days. You were sedated up until yesterday. Your body had some time to heal."

"Are you a doctor?"

He laughed. "Am I a doctor?" he chuckled. "Now, do I look like a doctor. No, I'm the guy that brought you here."

I shook my head, confused.

"I was coming back from searching for my brother in Jersey, I pulled over to stop and rest. Because it was dark and I was tired. Funny thing, maybe it wasn't funny, you were laying on the road. I thought you were a dead body when I passed you. Good thing I didn't run over you."

"So it was your car I climbed in. I thought it was abandoned"

Pete shook his head. "Nope it was mine. I got out to take a whiz and I see you coming toward the car."

"Why didn't you say anything."

"Dude, I saw you on the road, laying there, I thought dead as a doornail and then you're staggering, dragging your leg. I thought you were a zombie."

That made me laugh, because I remember feeling like one. I stifled the laugh when I realized it hurt.

"Then you climbed in the back of the car. I knew you weren't a dead thing when you threw that seat cover over you and were out. I got a good look." Pete whistled. "Ain't never seen anyone that bad. I knew I had to try to find you some help."

"Are you from around here?" I asked.

"Yep. Guys at our safety perimeter were shocked to see me pulling up at night, I can tell you," Pete said.

"So, I'm in a hospital?"

Pete leaned in and dropped his voice. "Actually, a vet clinic. But ..." he sat back. "It was the closest medical place to our camp set up and it had bandages. But you needed more. A lot more. Best we had was a paramedic Lou. You probably would have died. You should have died, but you had some angels or something looking out for you."

I grumbled. "Part of me wished they hadn't."

"I feel you. I do. But you're meant to survive, Buttercup. Look at the circumstances. I didn't run you over, when I should of. You got into my car. I got you here. You took a beating like no man I have ever seen, still walked a highway. And just as you're gasping at death's door, what do you know. A guy stops at one of our Quick Pit stations for gas. We don't let strangers have our gas, so of course, our guys gave him a hard time. But he tells us he needed it and he was ... ready ... a doctor."

"Holy cow."

"Lick of time, too," Pete said. "Best part?"

"He saved my life?" I asked.

"Not that, yeah, that probably was the best part, but that's not what I'm talking about."

"What are you talking about then?"

"Well, the guys told them about you and said they'd give him gas if he took a look," Pete said, "He did, and guess what? Not only could he try to help you, he knew you."

"He knew me?" I asked.

Pete nodded. "He said he thought he knew you, but you looked like the Barney the Dinosaur version of his friend."

"I believe ..." his voice entered the room. "My words were, he looked like a purple bloated version of my friend, Travis." He walked closer to the bed. "Hey, Travis."

I felt a sense of joy mixed in with relief when I saw Doctor Jon Yee standing before my bed. "It was you, Doc. You helped me?"

"It was me. Fate must really have plans for us. It had us together in the beginning," Jon said. "And it made sure I got to you before you reached the end."

"So ..." Pete swung his finger back and forth between us. "You two really do know each other?"

I answered, "Yes."

"Here I thought he was mistaken. I have to go tell the guys." He stood up. "We had a bet going. Glad you're on the mend," he said to me. "And glad I can call you Travis for sure." Without saying anymore, Pete hurriedly left.

"Why ... why would he think you were mistaken?" I asked.

"Honestly." Jon walked over and sat in Pete's chair. "You didn't look like you. In fact, you still look really bad. Travis ...

you could have died. You should have died. What the hell happened? Who beat you and why?"

"I'm not sure. But I have a feeling, in this world now, no one needs a reason to beat a man to a pulp. That's just sad and I'm not sure," I said. "It's the kind of world, I wanna be living in."

NINETEEN – FRANKLIN

An ageless ginger, that was how I would describe the nice woman who brought me a bowl of thin oatmeal, a cup of coffee and a set of clothes. Long dark ginger hair, smooth skin and freckles. Probably older than she looked, I always thought gingers just didn't age like the rest of us.

"I know what it's like to be on a ventilator," she said. "Everything is lukewarm. You should be able to tolerate it."

"Thank you," I replied.

"And the clothes aren't yours, but your clothes weren't salvageable."

"I understand, thank you again, ma'am."

"Do you need any help?" she asked.

"If you can wait outside that door, I'll call you if I do."

"That's where I'll be. Just ..." she pointed to the food. "Please try to eat."

I lifted the mug of coffee and took a sip, it was warm, and she was right, I probably wouldn't have handled anything hot.

The oatmeal looked and smelled good. She watched me pick up the spoon and take a bite. Supervising in a way, making sure I was gonna eat. Once she saw me eat a spoonful, she left me to finish then get dressed.

Jon had taken the IV out of my left arm, which made it easier to sit on the side of the bed and eat, getting dressed was going to be a bitch, everything hurt.

I could see the woman in the next room, she read a book, no

one else was around, but the place was set up like a mini hospital. Jon said the Franklin camp wanted things close and tight, everyone together, or else he probably would have had me at the medical center three miles away.

I respected Jon and his form of medicine, although I wasn't sure how much of that he used on me. He said I was in no shape to leave and for a few days he wanted me close to where there were medical supplies and equipment. They had the wedding hall connected to the church on the corner, some beds were set up there and that was where several people had set up their home.

Strangers that were in town, had passed through, even some that lived locally and didn't want to be alone.

Again, I believed it was all part of keeping people together. It seemed universal, an unspoken survival ritual. World ends, everyone that survived lives together.

Sweetwater had a center town camp, High Water survivors camped around Pastor Monroe's chapel.

I didn't get it. Go home.

Of course, who was I to judge, when I wasn't sleeping in my truck, I was on that park bench.

Since he arrived in town, Jon had been staying at the church. I'd go there too, to heal. He didn't blame me for not wanting to stay in a veterinarian clinic and he stated that he understood I probably wanted to go home, but he needed me to stay put.

I didn't tell him I didn't think I was welcome back in High Water, not yet, if at all.

Chief Fisher probably thought I died in one of those fires or took off somewhere to kill myself. Hell, I had been gone over a week. That's what I would think.

I finished off what I could of my breakfast and I managed to get my jeans on with some difficulty, my legs were achy and weak and standing up made me dizzy. I relied on the bed to accomplish that task, but getting that tee shirt over my head was tough, I had to call for the nice lady to help.

She did, then helped me get a long sleeved, jean shirt on as well.

"Those ribs will ache for a while," she said. "Try not to sleep on your back or flat because it's tough to get up for several weeks. And practice deep breathing, I know it hurts."

"You sound like you know about them. Did you break yours?"

She shook her head. "No. My husband did. Car accident, same one that landed me on the ventilator, like you, for just a few days. But that was … gosh, ten years ago. My how time flies. Have a seat, I'll tie those boots for you."

"You're very kind …."

"Angie," she said her name.

"You're very nice, Angie, I'm Travis."

"I know." She lifted my leg resting my boot on her thigh.

It made me smile and think of Maranda. "You know," I said. "This brings back memories. When the ARC virus hit a few years back. I had it."

"Did you?" Angie asked surprised. "I did, too."

"Oh, yeah? That's why you survived this."

"Yep." She set down my foot then grabbed the other.

"I forgot how to tie my shoes," I said.

"Now?"

"No, then. From the Arc virus. That's how I knew, I forgot how to tie them. Other things I forgot, I was able to learn again. Not the laces. Couldn't get it. No matter what I did or tried it was like trying to write Japanese."

She laughed. "Someone had to tie your shoes every day?"

"Yep."

"I would have found Velcro."

"That's exactly what my wife did."

"Smart woman."

"Yeah," I said peacefully. "She was. What about you? How did it affect you?"

"A couple ways, the biggest was my ability to write, but I also lost all memory of direction," she said. "I'd walk down a hall and not know how to get back. It was scary."

"I know. Your husband, did he make it?"

"Actually, he did." She set my foot down. "He was adamant about not getting the vaccine. Said he didn't have the Alzheimer gene and wasn't getting it."

"That's good. Good for you."

"What about your wife, Travis?" she asked.

I shook my head. "She didn't make it. My two kids either."

"I'm very sorry," she spoke compassionately.

"Did ... do ... you have kids?"

"Before all this ... no. Now I have five."

"Five?" I spat in shock. "How do you get five kids in a month?"

"All little ones that didn't get the vaccine yet. Some of us were pretty fast around here finding those kids."

"Wait, they get the shot at two," I said. "That has to be five very young kids."

"They are."

"That's very kind of you."

"We aren't the only ones who took in little ones," she said. "Lots did. We all have to do our part. I'm sure you did."

"I didn't. Not while my family was sick, I didn't."

"Well, that's understandable."

"Man, you are a very nice woman."

She smiled gently. "Any reason not to be?"

"People find reasons."

"Like the ones that did this to you?" she asked. "I'm sorry this happened."

"Me, too."

"Well, I have to go. We're salvaging summer wear for folks. I'll try to get you a few more tee shirts."

"Thank you."

She grabbed my bowl and cup, gave me one more smile and left me alone.

I sat on the bed ready to go. I could see a bit of the church when I looked out the window next to my bed, but wasn't sure if I was supposed to just go there or not and I forgot to ask Angie.

After finishing off my glass of water, I figured it was time to try. Holding on to the bed, I slowly stood up right.

I was stone cold sober, but felt like I was drunk. My head had that woozy feeling and the room spun a little. I gave it time to pass, felt stable and took a step. A pain shot from my knee, up my leg to my hip and I cringed. I hadn't even put all my weight forward.

The phrase 'hurt with every step I took' was going to apply to me.

Hand on the bed for support, I inched forward.

"Whoa, hey," Jon called out, rushing in. "Where are you going?"

"I thought we were going to the church to rest."

"We are. We are." Jon placed his hand on my arms. "But you aren't doing it alone. I have a wheel chair for you."

"You have to be shitting me," I said. "A wheelchair? I don't need one."

"For now you do. Sit down. I'll get it. It's in the waiting room. Sit." He guided me to the bed.

I sat down. "All this fuss to get me across the street."

"We'll get there," Jon said. "But first, Duncan wants to see you. Don't move." He stepped away. "I'll be right back."

My new friend hurried away and that was when what he said hit me.

"Duncan?" I asked. "Who the hell is Duncan?"

<><><><>

When I last saw the note it was pitch black, now I had the chance to see it in the light. Yellow paper, crinkled and blood stained. When Jon said I was meeting Duncan, then explained that Duncan was the leader of the group, I assumed Duncan was a man.

Boy, was I surprised to see a middle-aged woman handing me that letter. We met with her at a table in an empty coffee shop. It seemed as if it were her office. She wore blue jeans and a canvas jacket.

"This was on you," she said. "What do you know about it?"

"Not much," I replied. "All I know is when I was on the road it was on my chest. I don't know what it says."

"It's a warning to us not to send anyone else," Duncan replied. "The Nashville group has control of all the food in the area, the distribution centers. They set up camp around the Costco. Two of our people joined their group to get some food."

"A guy named Ryan?" I asked.

Duncan nodded. "Yeah, how did you know?"

"It's was one of the names they mentioned when they were kicking my ass."

"They obviously thought you were one of us."

"Pete told me you control the gas around here," I said. "Is that true?"

"It is."

"So, they have the food, you have the gas. Do you beat people up for taking the gas?" I asked. "Because it seems to me the solution is first grader simple … share."

After a short hum out, she sat back and folded her hands. "I wish it were that simple. We are not the only camps that are taking control."

"You know when they were beating me up, all I kept thinking of was those apocalypse movies with gangs and how, you know, I never thought it would get like that."

Jon added, "Sadly it is, the bigger the cities, the worse it is. That's why I left Vegas. Ever see the Stand?"

"Can't say that I have," I replied.

"Well, then ..." Jon cleared his throat. "That analogy won't work."

"It's lawlessness," said Duncan. "Pure and simple."

"I don't get why. Maybe I live in some fairy tale world, but it's only been a month. What the heck are people doing? Seventy percent of the country is dead, probably more with those who killed themselves or died by assholes like the ones that beat me up." I shook my head. 'Does anyone have an answer?"

"I can try to explain," she said. "At least my opinion."

"Please do," I told her.

"Say you eat a can of beans. When is the next time you'll get another can? When you go to the store, maybe pick clean a neighbor? Eventually those cans will go bad or run out. Fuel, you think there are going to be any more plants? Anyone drilling? Not for a while."

I shook my head. "I'm not a math genius, and I don't take credit for this, but my friend Joe Randal said that even with seventy percent gone, we still have more people than a hundred and fifty years ago. They did just fine farming food."

"Farmers? Well, I hope some survived," she said. "But I am willing to wager any farmers, and farmland will be part of the hubs, they sent us a list of locations, and all of them center around farm areas. They'll be secure. Yep, the government and their continuity of life and law is out there." She looked up. "Power is on because they are sending people to the grids. Won't be for long. Those people will focus on the hubs."

"Even if the lights will go out here?" I asked. "You folks aren't going?"

"I really don't want to be part of whatever government camps they are setting up. They'll fall eventually," she said.

"Maybe they won't," I argued. "You don't know."

"A lot of people don't know," she replied, "You asked for an explanation, Travis, I'm not saying I'm right, I'm just giving you my opinion. You asked why we don't share? Those of us who have, are holding on. Bartering will be the way of life, those who have commodities have life."

"So, you hold on with greed hoping the other guy don't get it? That's just ... the world ended, why can't we bury the bad?"

"Your goodness and naivety are refreshing and I pray you hold on to that," she said. "The world needs a voice of reason. But history shows this is what happens. When the Black Plague wiped out seventy-five percent of Europe, society broke down. Gangs, thieves, murderers, it was hard to keep law and order when law and order was dead."

"Yeah, that's not fair," I said. "Things were already rough when the Black Plague hit."

She raised an eyebrow. "And they weren't already bad when the ARC effect happened? I think you know the answer to this. The only difference is, those who remained in the government have been trying to build it back up. I hope they do. Until I know that course, I stay mine."

"Thank you. So, why did you want to see me?" I asked. "Was it just about that letter?"

"Actually, I don't need to ask you anymore, I have my answer," she said. "We wanted to know if you were planning or needed help in retaliation? You did take a beating because of us. But I can see, that's not who you are."

"No, it's not."

"Will you be staying on with us after you heal?" she asked.

"Not sure I have any real skill sets to contribute," I told her. "Honestly, I worked in a print shop. I appreciate your hospitality though."

Jon stood and walked behind my wheelchair. "We need to get him back to bed and rested."

"I understand," she said. "Travis, I hope this world doesn't change you too much, you seem like a good person."

I only nodded a thanks, but inside I knew she was wrong. How could the world not have changed me already? I lost everything. And as far as being a good person, I was at one time. To me, I stopped being a good person the moment I put that pillow to Maranda's face, and if that didn't do it, burning those buildings in High Water did.

TWENTY – THINK ABOUT IT

Some religions called it a sacristy, some called it a vestry, since I was born and raised Catholic and I was healing in a Baptist church, I didn't know what it was called. It was this room behind the altar and a strange place to hang out and get better.

When I was an altar boy for all of four months, it was the place we'd get ready. This room was a bit different. A white cross with no Jesus on it hung on the wall, other than that it could have been for storage. It was hard to tell because things were moved around to make way for two narrow twin beds.

It was better than the veterinary clinic, warm and soothing.

I wasn't sure if it was the room or the fact that I knew I was in a house of worship that made me feel calm.

"Good?" Jon asked, adjusting my covers.

"Yep. I feel like I am some sort of summer bible camp."

"Oh, yeah?" Jon said. "Did you go to those?"

"No, I was Catholic, we didn't do the bible thing."

Jon smiled. "Now, I'm not gonna hook you up to an IV unless you aren't getting enough fluids."

"I appreciate this. I actually feel pretty good."

"I'm sure. Tomorrow we'll walk from this room to the entrance of the church and you tell me how you feel."

"I'm sure I'll be fine."

"I'm sure you think that. You haven't had to really exert yourself."

"I don't see how driving or riding in a car is exerting yourself."

"It's not exertion," Jon said. "As much as what if there is trouble? A few hours in a car is a long time. Now, Angie is gonna come in with your lunch, check your vitals for me. Believe it or not, I actually have some patients to see."

"Do they know you do that Eastern Western Medicine?" I asked.

Jon laughed. "Eastern Medicine or Traditional Chinese, and yes, but I know the other stuff too."

"Did you use that on me? The Traditional Chinese medicine?"

"I ... I did. For what I could, the bruising, the broken bones."

"Well, heck that must work magic because I feel really good."

"Again, because you're not exerting yourself. Travis, you fractured your skull."

"I suppose I did. You know this town probably would love to have you stay, being a doctor and all."

"They mentioned it."

"And those hubs. Bet if you went there, you'd get prime everything," I said.

"Do you want to go to one of those hubs? I mean there's a list of places."

I shrugged. "Maybe."

"You know Travis," he sat down on the bed next to mine. "When they told me they had a severely injured man, I didn't recognize you at first. You were so badly beaten and bloody. Then when I did figure out I knew you, I thought you had a death wish and that was what happened. You tried to die. Is that true?"

"You mean did I get beat that bad on purpose? Did I piss someone off so they'd do that? No." I shook my head.

"Okay, I was just curious because you didn't and haven't mentioned about going back to High Water."

"That's because I'm not real sure I am welcome back there."

"What do you mean?" he asked. "Did something happen?"

"You can say I sort of burned the place."

"What? What do you mean you burned the place?"

"They had been storing the dead in two buildings and every day it was the same thing. Take out a few bodies, bury them. We weren't making progress and every day it got harder, the bodies smelled more and they were just sticky, disgusting messes of people we knew."

"So you burned down the two buildings?"

I nodded.

"Why didn't you just say you weren't going to help?"

"Because they already thought I was some sort of louse for not lifting a finger when my family was sick. So I helped after my family passed."

"And you don't think they think you're an even bigger louse now?" he asked.

"Wow, that was harsh."

"Look, what you did, they're doing all over the country. Maybe," Jon said. "They're more grateful than angry. Maybe they're glad you had the balls to do something they didn't. They weren't moving forward until the dead were buried."

"Somehow, I don't know, they aren't those type of people. I've known them my whole life."

"And they have known you." Jon stood. "We'll go to the hub if you want. But you have to go home. At least to your home. I'm sure there are things you need and want to take."

I shook my head. "Nah, I'm good. I actually haven't been back in my house since Daisy died."

"When did Daisy pass?"

"When I left town it was three weeks."

"So a month?" Jon asked. "You haven't stepped foot in your own home for a month? Can I ask why?"

"It's painful, Doc," I replied. "Going home, going in there, it's filled with memories."

"Exactly. And that's why you need to go home."

"The memories are too hard," I said.

"The memories are all you got. What is the first thing that went for them? For everyone? Their ability to think and remember." Jon shook his head. "I have to go, I'll be back. But ponder this, what a tragedy and disservice it is to those we loved not to honor them every day with the one thing they lost and we still have... the one thing that keeps them alive .... memories. Think about it," he said. "Because you still can."

<><><><>

I had met some genuinely nice people in my life, but Angie surely had to be one of the nicest. Although when I looked at her, she didn't have that broken look like so many of us had, even Duncan had that look. Angie, like Jon Yee, didn't really lose anyone. Which was a blessing because they are able to help people without feeling a bitterness.

Maybe it's just me who felt the bitterness.

I really did feel stronger and better, but Jon was right. I wasn't really exerting myself as any test. Until I had to search out the restroom. It was close, but because I didn't know the building, I walked around a bit.

By the time I got there, I was dizzy and had to hold on to the sink for support. That's when I saw my face, I barely recognized myself.

Half my face was swollen and distorted, my top lip was split and a few sutures held it together. I looked like a purple and blue monster, the whites of my eyes were beyond bloodshot they were red.

I couldn't believe I took that bad of a beating. Lifting my shirt showed me how much more punishment my body endured. By the time I stumbled my way to a stall and did my business, I was done. I made it out of the restroom, held on to the wall and slid down to the floor. My energy was gone, head hurt, and I was too dizzy to go on.

Angie found me.

She was looking for me and had brought me some pain medication and a late lunch. She helped me to my feet then back to my bed.

Propping the pillow behind me, Angie aided me in sitting up. Next to my bed was a plate with some bread and a mug with a spoon.

"Do you need me to feed you?" she asked.

"No, I'll manage."

"You need to eat."

"I will. Especially since I just found out how difficult it is to get food."

"Well, we have food. Just getting more from what's out there is the problem." She handed me the mug. "It's canned stew so it's not some gourmet meal."

"I appreciate it." I took the mug. "Food and gas. Anything else people are being territorial over?"

"Medicine, weapons," she stated. "There are about four or five groups in the Nashville area."

"Gangs, you mean," I said.

"I think people are confused and scared. Just scared that they won't have anything tomorrow or next week."

"What about the hubs?" I asked. "Have you thought about going?"

"I have. I mean we have the five children. I know Duncan thought about sending some people to check them out, you know for those who may want to go."

"So she'd let you go?"

Angie snickered. "This isn't a prison, silly. Duncan has a plan. Protect the commodities in this town, have bartering power with the Hubs. That still doesn't mean I'm staying. I'm just thinking of what's best for the kids. What about you? I'm sure once you woke up you just wanted to go home."

I shrugged, not knowing how to respond to that.

"What were you doing in Nashville? Was it just to get food?" she asked.

"I was running."

"From?"

"Life. Death. Mistakes."

"I got news for you Travis, you can run from here to California," she said. "You can't ever run from any of those things. Because they are right here." She reached out and touched my chest. "Right there. Sometimes the answer isn't running, sometimes it's just staying put and facing it."

She stayed and chatted awhile. We spoke about life and family, then I took a nap.

I woke for a little more and then took another nap. I couldn't believe how tired I was. I also couldn't believe how much time had passed since my daughter died and I left High Water.

My head was spinning and not just from the head injury.

I was still filled with such intense grief, and now I was also in immense physical pain, as well. I looked like a bad stand for Rocky after the Creed fight.

I was a sorry excuse for a person.

But I was like so many people. They may not have gotten their asses kicked physically, but emotionally they were all in the same boat.

I didn't know what to make of my awakening and all that I learned during the course of the day.

I did know one thing.

After my morning talk with Jon and afternoon conversation with Angie, it was time.

It was no 'one' thing that was said, it was just a realization that I made.

When I was physically ready it truly was time. Even if my final decision was to find one of the hubs, before I did that, it was time to face the consequences of my actions, my losses and go home.

TWENTY-ONE – THE RETURN

April 9

Someone said it was Easter. I didn't know how they would know that or even why. I was certain when we arrived back in High Water Pastor Monroe would know.

I had a few setbacks in Franklin. Jon being a doctor was my godsend, the headaches, the brain bleed. It was a good thing that the last scan he did of my head was clear because the power went down the next day.

There was a warning, a three-day warning. It came over the radio and all working cell phones.

An annoying buzzing and the message flashed like an Amber Alert.

As of April first, all power will be diverted to the hubs. Residents not within a hundred miles of a hub will no longer have access to cell towers.

It was a blatant attempt to get people to the hubs.

I didn't get it at first, then Jon, on the drive explained to me why it was or in his opinion why he thought it was.

"Civilization, obviously, is not dead," Jon said. "However, the more people they have organized, under one government, the more they can cultivate a society. There will be leaders within each division, but if Duncan and the others don't join a hub, they'll be like, I don't know, their own countries and they don't have what it takes to survive. Sure they have food, gas, but you need other things."

"I get it. I just … why do they have to have these hubs? Why can't they just let people be where they are?"

"Dude, you got beat up outside a Costco distribution center in East Franklin, right now, do you think that's gonna work? Do you think the pilgrims were like, 'hey, here's the land go anywhere you want'."

"I'm not sure I want to live in a hub whatever that is," I told him.

"We'll find out, won't we?"

"Did you bring that list?"

"It came as an alert on the phone," Jon replied, then turned his head to look out his window.

I knew why.

It happened again, the fifth or sixth time on our three hour drive. Another car drove by us.

I hadn't seen another car sharing the highway with me in a long time, nor had I seen a plane, yet two of them flew overhead. Both low flying and both twin engines.

The car that passed us had to be doing ninety, Jon was cruising at a good speed.

The planes, the cars, the people were signs of life. Life moving on.

I still didn't understand how people could do that. I was nowhere near gaining any ambition to live, to keep going.

I was thinking about that when the Amber Alert sounding buzz came from Jon's phone. I hurriedly reached for mine from the bag at my feet. I had shut it off when signals were lost and now I immediately powered it back up.

"I have a signal," I said looking at my phone. "We must be within a hundred miles."

"What does the alert say?"

"It's a warning," I read. "Lists areas to avoid as dangerous zones and highways not to take."

"Don't tell me High Water is one of them?"

"No." I shook my head. "But Nashville is."

"You heard Duncan. There are four big groups out there," Jon said.

"You spent more time with them than I did. Does Franklin have a leg to stand on against these guys?"

"Sadly," Jon shook his head. "No."

"I hope Duncan and the others find a hub. There were some nice people in that town."

"From what we saw."

"What do you mean?" I asked.

"I mean, Travis, you were beaten as a warning to them. Violence invokes violence. I'm gonna go out on a limb and say the folks in Franklin aren't all that innocent. But hey ..." He reached over and tapped my hand that held the phone. "We're close to a hub and High Water. Who knows maybe High Water is the hub?"

I wanted to tell him that I doubted that very much. High Water wasn't big enough nor near any farming or industrial areas to be a hub.

A part of me wondered though when we drove by Reilly's and I saw the front door was boarded up. Not the way I remembered leaving it. Reilly's was my daily pit stop. Maybe the government had gone in. But I soon learned that was not the case. All that nervous energy that stirred in my belly in anticipation of returning home was for naught.

High Water was a ghost town.

Not a person that we could see. The sight of Reilly's made me sad. If it really was Easter, it was evident by the church, Pastor Monroe had that locked up tight.

Jon slowed down and stopped at the edge of town when we arrived at the Municipal Building.

"You weren't kidding, were you?" he opened up the car door and stepped out. "You set it aflame, someone else finished the job."

Only the Municipal Building sign remained. It perched on the small patch of grass before the walkway that led to the building.

The white brick building was a heap of rubble. Some of the

bricks were soot covered and was the only indication that it had caught fire and not just demolished.

But someone had knocked the building down.

I wondered if they did it after or to put out the flames and smother it.

We got back in the car and drove a little farther just past the grocery store, before we stopped again.

I likened the town to renters leaving an apartment. There were two types, that ones that made things look tidy and the others that left a mess.

Chief Fisher and the others tidied the town, readied it for the next tenant.

That told me they weren't dead or anything, would thugs and marauders leave a town cleaned up?

Every single store front window on the main street was boarded up with fresh plywood. It was exceptionally neat. Nothing looked busted or vandalized.

"Wow," I exhaled the word staring at Terri's boarded up bookstore. "They sure had enough initiative to do this in three weeks but couldn't for the dead."

"Maybe they didn't do this alone," Jon suggested. "You said there were what? Twelve?'

"Ten, after the two suicides. But twelve people didn't do this. I mean, they could have gotten some help from Sweet Water."

"Or the hub." Jon pulled out his phone. "There are two hub cities in Tennessee, Jackson and Marysville. Which one is nearer?"

"Marysville is about thirty miles away," I answered. "Maybe that's where they went."

"Maybe this is what they do when you agree to join. Or ... your town just wants to come back home one day. Looks like they prepared for a hurricane. So ..." He put away his phone. "Let's head to your street."

"This is my street."

"You live on the main drag?"

"I live ..." I turned and pointed to the building behind me.

Almost in shock, Jon looked at my home. "Maranda's Magic."

"My wife's gallery," I said. "We bought this building and redid the whole thing. We lived above. It is a kick ass apartment."

"Must have cost you a fortune."

"Every cent we had ... but at least we didn't pay for labor. I did all the work myself."

"That's pretty impressive and ..." Jon pointed. "They boarded the windows. They can't hate you that much."

"Which leads me to believe maybe the hub people did do it."

"You ready to go in?"

"No. But ..." I looked at my building. "It's time."

It was baby steps back into my life, back into everything that showed me what I had lost. It was so hard to believe my entire family had died six weeks earlier, all within days of each other.

I truly wasn't ready for it and was happy Jon was with me. It wasn't a step I wanted to take alone.

When Daisy died, I was done.

For those weeks before being beaten to a pulp I questioned my existence, why would I want to live in a world without my family?

When I survived the attack, I wondered why. Why was I destined to live?

We entered the building through Maranda's gallery. No death occurred there, it was her work.

I wasn't even thinking about the art when we stepped in. It was hard to see anything, the only light came through the door. "We can go through here, there's a back staircase that goes to the apartment. I have an LED light in the back. Had it for Maranda in case power went out in the middle of her working."

"Oh, Travis," Jon said with wonder. "Can you get it now? I mean, unless you want to just remove the boards on the windows."

"For what?"

"For this, my friend. This is amazing."

It was then I noticed he was enthralled at the sight of the paintings that hung along with her statues, all on display in a gallery her and I designed.

"I understand the boarded windows protecting this," Jon said. "But it does not deserve to be in the dark."

Maybe I had seen it so much it lost the impact it had given to Jon.

Immediately I walked to the back, grabbed the LED light and the hammer, gave Jon the light and stepped outside. The board was put up in a hurry, four nails, one in each corner. It didn't take much to take the first board down. I rested it against the building and walked back inside.

And with the light of the day, I was able to see the magic that my wife had created.

"There are those who would envy this," Jon told me. "All this work. Travis, you know..." he faced me. "It is said that when a person dies their soul goes elsewhere to some supernatural plane, whatever name it is given. But ... It's hard for me to believe that Maranda's soul transcended any plane."

"Wow, that's not encouraging."

"No," Jon chuckled. "I mean, it's hard to imagine her anywhere else because her soul is right here. It's everywhere. Feel it Travis, just ... feel it."

He was right, they weren't just Maranda's paintings, they were a part of her, an extension of her being. I had mourned my wife so deeply, I had forgotten how easy it was to feel her again.

The first step back into my home was a lesson I needed to learn.

<><><><>

There was a smell to my home, not one of death as it was when I left it. The lingering scent of loss was one of the reasons

I hated to return, that and everywhere I turned was a memory that stabbed me in the heart.

Nothing had been touched.

Dishes were still in the sink, Daisy's blanket was folded over the back of the couch, and my bed was stripped, bed dismantled and mattress propped up against the wall.

Things that I had done.

My home was just the way I left it.

Things looked the same but they didn't feel the same. It was missing the buzz of familiarity and soul.

It was returning to the apartment that made me realize in a way, I had come full circle.

When I found the building seven years earlier it was a shell that needed so much work, and I had to decide whether I wanted to take on the task or not. Did I want to start from scratch and make something out of it, make a life there?

Now I stood in the building, and I, not the building was the empty shell, it represented how void of everything I was. I was the one that needed so much work. Once again, I had to decide if I wanted to take on the task or walk away.

It was time to make a choice, I knew it and felt it coming. It wasn't fair to myself to spend each day deciding if I was going to strike my last match.

I had been in some sort of life limbo trying to figure out what I was going to do.

It boiled down to live or die.

If I decided I wanted to work on living, then I had to find a way to make it a life.

Maybe it was too soon and I was putting too much pressure on myself. I did know, if I made the decision to live, then I had to bring life back, not only to myself but to that apartment. Because the apartment like me, felt dead inside.

<><><><>

We didn't stay at my place long, my choice not Jon's. I thought since I was feeling better and Marysville wasn't that far away, we would see what the hub cities truly entailed. If I were going to make a decision on what I was going to do, I needed all the facts.

What was Marysville like now and were those from High Water there, or did they all just go to other places?

Another car passed us on the route there, we definitely were headed to the right place.

In my mind I envisioned a military blockage set up and some sort of FEMA camp thing on the edge of town. In reality, there was nothing stopping us. No one telling us what to do or where to go. We rolled over the small bridge into town and it had the buzz of a busy Saturday afternoon.

There was a good bit of traffic, people slowing down, trying to find a place to park on the street. Folks walking around like lost tourists carrying their belongings.

We drove just as slow, like those before us, we didn't really have a plan.

"There." Jon pointed to a man and a little boy. The boy had a backpack and the man shouldered a duffel bag. "I saw them getting directions. Talking to someone." He stopped the car and rolled down the window. "Excuse me," he called to them.

The man stopped.

"Hey, hi," Jon said. "Is there somewhere we go if we just got here?"

The man replied. "Just up the street is the Municipal Building. At least that's what I was told. I heard there's a parking lot there, you might be able to go around the block."

"Thank you. Good luck." Jon wound up the window and looked at me. "The Municipal Building. Don't get any funny ideas."

"Ha." I nodded my head in a point. "Turn left up here to go around."

We inched our way to the intersection, pausing for people

to cross the street. When we turned the bend, I saw a church. It was a beautiful spring day and the front yard of the church had a large crowd of people, it looked like a picnic of sorts. Then I saw the sign out front welcoming everyone to Easter Services.

There was a different feel in the town of Marysville. One that could be seen and sensed. It was fresh and didn't have that town in mourning feel like High Water and Sweet Water, nor did it have that Apocalypse survivor feel of Franklin.

We made our way around the block locating the Municipal Building and courthouse. After finding a spot in the lot, Jon turned off the car and looked at me. "What's the plan?"

"What do you mean?"

"You suggested we come here. Are we just inquiring or did you see your home and decide to run away again?"

"That is not fair. I just ... I just wanted to see, you know. See what's here. I'm still trying to figure out what I'm going to do."

"About what, Travis?" Jon asked. "No one says you have to decide anything right now. You can go with the flow. Do what you want. But I think you know what you want."

"What if I don't. I mean, does anyone? What do you want? Do you even know what you want out of this world now?" I questioned.

"Yeah, I don't want to be alone. I want to be useful and if I was chosen for some reason to survive a really fucked up, clean slate situation, then I want to be a part of making everything better." He stepped out of the car.

"You thought about that answer, didn't you?" I got out as well and followed.

"No."

"That did not just come off the top of your head."

"Why not? Just because I know what I want?" Jon said, as we approached the building. "I think you also know what you want, Travis, but just can't verbalize what your heart is telling you. And it's not a death wish."

"Huh?"

Jon stopped and faced me. "You don't have a death wish,

Travis, even though I said it. No one who has a death wish fights so hard to live."

"Does that traditional Chinese medicine come with a book of wisdom?" I asked, opening the door to the Municipal Building. "Cause you're awfully wise."

"Thanks and yes, actually, yes, it does. It's part of the graduation process."

"Oh, you're just fooling me." I stopped the second we went inside, I couldn't believe all the people in there. Lines of folding tables were set up. Men and women sat behind them. It looked like an entire registration area.

In fact, it was.

We saw the man and his son from the street sitting at a table with a man, they were being handed paperwork.

Listening to the meshed voices, I picked out bits and pieces of what was being said. Names, background information, where they came from.

"This way." Jon tugged me and led me down the hall way to an available table where a woman sat as if waiting, she had a small laptop before her.

"Hello, new arrivals?" she asked.

Jon answered, "Yes."

"Have a seat," she instructed.

"Busy, huh?" I asked, sitting down.

"Steady. People are just starting to arrive so we're a little chaotic." She handed us each a folder. "You'll need to fill out the paperwork and turn it in at your temporary camp. We are organizing people by skills and getting them situated in housing that way. Until now, we have temporary housing out at the airport. Let me get your names and I'll get you a unit number."

"Jon Yee," he said.

She typed. "And your occupation, Mister Yee."

"Physician."

"Oh," she said brightly. "Area of specialty?"

"General Practitioner."

"And," I added. "He knows Traditional Chinese medicine."

"Wonderful, and you?" she asked.

"Travis Grady, and I don't really have any skill set. I worked in a print shop."

"Are you kidding me?" Jon laughed. "You renovated and remodeled an entire old building ... alone. That's skill."

"That's not skill," I argued. "It's a hobby. Not a skill."

"I beg to differ. And ... someone who doesn't have skill would be like a social influencer. Someone that spent their entire day making game videos and trying to influence people. Imagine coming in here and saying that."

"We have one," the woman said. "We actually put her as community rep."

"I stand corrected," Jon said.

"Builder." She tapped. "I'll put you as a builder, Mr. Grady."

The interview process was short, she gave us a bracelet, unit number and directions to the small airport. I still didn't know what the heck we were doing, I knew right away, Jon was going to have much more importance in the town than me, just by the wrist band they gave him. His was blue. Mine was white as were the bracelets on most people I saw.

That vision I had of a military camp came to fruition when we arrived at the airport.

Multitudes of white trailers lined up neatly like a crowded trailer park. Each section marked as a unit and each unit had a check in tent.

We filled out our paperwork, turned it in and were given a trailer number. If we needed anything we were to ask. We were also told since Jon was a doctor, he'd be given housing within a day or two.

It was all kind of whirlwind. Two hours from the time we arrived in Marysville we were inside a cramped trailer and Jon was being asked if he could visit the clinic and check in there.

I went with him figuring I would see what was happening in town, since heading back to High Water seemed to be removed as an option for the day. It worried me, was it like a prison? Would I even be able to leave?

It all seemed too planned, too regimented.

But even with that, one thing was certain, Marysville was full of life.

Everyone seemed generally happy. What had they found in the aftermath of their loss that I hadn't?

"You okay?" Jon asked.

"Yeah, it's just weird. That trailer is weird."

"Considering we spent weeks living in a room behind an altar the trailer seems to be a nice change of pace. Then again ..." Jon stopped walking. "Your apartment would be a great change of pace. Fix it up, do the dishes."

"Can we even leave?"

Jon laughed. "You act like we signed our life away."

"They just rushed us around."

"They have a process, that's all and ..."

"Travis?" My name was called. "Jesus, Travis is that you?"

I knew that voice and I was almost apprehensive about turning around, but I did. Sure enough, Chief Fisher walked my way.

"Oh my God, you're alive." He rushed to me, placing his hands on my arms and gripping them. "Were you in an accident?"

"You can say that," I replied. "Thankfully my friend, Jon, here, saved me."

"I remember you," Chief Fisher said to Jon. "You were there that day with George."

"I was. Nice to see you Chief," Jon replied.

"Travis where the hell did you go?" Chief Fisher asked. "We really thought you were dead. We looked for you all over."

"You did?" I asked shocked. "I wouldn't think you would. I mean, I thought for sure you would hate me and think good riddance, after what I did with the funeral home and stuff."

"We were angry." Chief Fisher nodded. "We were really pissed at you. But we were still worried, had your truck not been gone we would have thought you died in the fires."

"I'm sorry, Chief. I am. I was out of my head and ..."

"No." he cut me off. "No. We were mad, and you had no right

to take it into your own hands. Not to mention it was really dangerous to us all. But after the fires ended and after a couple days of not being in the same sad rut, we knew it was for the best."

"Thank you," I said.

"Are you all here?" Jon asked. "Those who survived from High Water?"

"Almost," Chief answered. "Joe Randal is working on High Water. He'll pitch in here, but live there. For the rest of us. It's all still new. We've only been here about a week. We spent the last week boarding up High Water, keep in good shape in case we decide to go back. One day, hopefully we will. I mean let's face it, Travis, High Water is home. We can have a new place here, but all the memories are there. Can't go forward without embracing what you loved in the past."

"Wow," Jon said. "That's even better than things I've said."

"Thanks." The Chief winked. "I've been saying it a lot."

"So, Joe is in High Water?" I asked. "Or living there. Part of the Hub, but kind of commuting?"

"That's the plan."

"Ha. How about that." I nodded at Jon.

"What about you?" Fisher asked. "What's your plan?"

Jon laughed. "Travis said he doesn't have a plan."

"But you ..." I pointed to Jon. "You said I did but I wasn't listening to my heart. I think I finally hear it. You're right, Chief. We can't move forward without embracing what we loved in the past."

"Gonna commute like Joe?" Jon asked.

"Yeah. I'll see what I can do to help out here, but I need my family back," I said. "The only way to do that is to find them at home."

TWENTY-TWO – FULL CIRCLE

August 3

There really was no magical moment that swept over me and told me what the right path was to take. Many times over the course of the six month downfall of life, I believed I knew what I had to do and each time it just ended up being a stepping stone to a journey's end still yet, unknown.

That day in Marysville when I decided I needed to be home, needed to find a way to be around my family, it wasn't 'bam, this is it', it went through many evolutions.

I needed to see what Marysville had to offer, what made Joe Randal think the whole 'hub' city was good enough to be a part of but not live there.

It took me two weeks to find out it was a loss of freedom and self-expression.

Many people liked that. They moved forward to a new way of life so they didn't wallow in the sadness of the old.

To me, the only sadness there was in my past was losing what I loved.

Every other moment and minute were worth replaying like an old home movie.

I couldn't be like that, be this follower who did the same thing every single day, like a robot, like the days of picking up the dead in High Water.

People were happy, they had something to do, food for the

belly and medical care if needed. There had to be more.

Oddly enough, me being a builder meant squat, but me being a printer was a big deal and it played in my ability to live in High Water and be a productive member of Marysville.

I went back to the print shop all alone. I was responsible for printing all the paperwork, school worksheets and weekly newsletters.

Because the print shop was in High Water, we had power. It worked out great for me, Joe, Terri and a couple others who decided to live there.

I ran the printing jobs well and was pretty social at first. Going back and forth to Marysville quite a bit. I even took a drive to Franklin, despite danger warnings from the government.

Franklin was still surviving, but they were nothing like Marysville, no power, no medical, food supply was low and they had loss of life due to the constant battles with Nashville.

I led a small caravan of folks from Franklin to Marysville, it included Angie, her husband and their five kids.

Marysville was safer for them. To me though, it was a dystopian society masked as a Pleasantville world.

It looked pretty but it was just .... a gray society.

There was no money, so there were no rich, no poor, no classes. Everyone was the same, given the same distribution with vouchers for extras when earned.

That wasn't necessarily true and I saw that first hand. Jon was treated differently; his rations were better than mine. I didn't tell people, it wasn't my place, especially when Jon shared a lot with me.

Eventually, other than meeting with Jon, I stopped going to Marysville, and they came for their printing. I focused on High Water, more so my apartment.

I may have heard my heart that day in Marysville, but it took hearing my soul to know what my plan had to be.

Remembering.

Maranda's gallery was open and even if no one ever came, it

was there, in case someone wanted to meet my wife. I had taken everything of my children, wife and family and created a shrine in the living room. Pictures, drawings, papers, graded homework assignments, anything and everything, covered every inch of the walls.

So, each day it was a reminder of a life I would never forget.

It was my way to come home and see them, as if they were still alive.

I spent my days at the print shop working, while always reciting memories in my mind.

Spending an extended amount of time alone was what I preferred. Too many interactions with others took away from the world I created that kept me going.

I could be labeled insane, but I was alive and as long as I remembered them, so was my family.

In a way I lived in the past, but I had to.

We all had to.

Not only were we given the chance to live, we were given the ability to remember our lives, those we lost, the love and joy they gave us.

To stop living, to stop remembering would be wrong.

Because every single living being on the planet that lost their lives to the ARC vaccine reaction, were robbed of something special and precious.

Their memories.

For as long as I remained on the earth, I would carry my family with me through the countless memories they gave me.

It was not only the least I could do, it was what I wanted to do.

It kept me going.

Life goes on in different ways. Not always easy, not always fair, we just have to find our own way.

Finally, I did.

When I told Jon what I was doing, my wise doctor friend said to me, 'You don't get over a loss if you live in the past. You have to be able to move forward to get on with life and relationships.'

He was right.

However, I wasn't living in the past, I was just keeping the memory of it alive.

FROM THE AUTHOR

Thank you so much for reading this book.

Please visit my website www.jacquelinedruga.com and sign up for my mailing list for updates, freebies, new releases and give-aways. And, don't forget my Kindle club!

Your support is invaluable to me. I welcome and respond to your feedback. Please feel free to email me at Jacqueline@jacquelinedruga.com

BOOKS BY THIS AUTHOR

Flight 3430

In a small Montana town, it takes four minutes for every man, woman and child to die.

It isn't a virus or biological attack, but rather the beginning of a geological event that triggers a chain reaction across the globe with devastating effects.

A repeat of an extinction event that occurred millions of years earlier.

There is no stopping it. The only way to survive is to stay ahead of it.

Tom Foster hasn't flown in decades, yet, he sets his fear aside for a vacation with his grown sons. When the global catastrophe begins, Tom and his sons are in the safest place they could possibly be ... thirty thousand feet above the ground.

No matter the sacrifice, keeping his family alive is his number one priority and the only way to do that ... is not to land until it is safe.

With billions dying on the ground, it's a race to achieve the impossible because there is no other alternative if they want to live.

Rise

It starts as a fever.

A debilitating virus emerges in India and quickly burns its way through the densely populated areas of Asia. The victims suffer for days even weeks on end until finally succumbing. Streets are empty and major cities are mere graveyards

Because of the slow killing nature of the virus, attempts to contain it to one continent seemingly work at first, but human smuggling into infection-free areas cause the virus to break borders globally.

Darren Reynolds is a foot doctor and survival enthusiast. For years he has made it a hobby to collect all things survival, knowledge and goods. Despite the fact that the United States is fortress America, he knows the virus won't stay out forever. When news breaks that the virus is on American soil, he is ready to hunker down. He will do anything to protect his family from what threatens to wipe out mankind.

But Darren soon learns, things aren't what they seem. The threat of man's extinction will not come from the virus. It will come from what rises in the aftermath.

Printed in Great Britain
by Amazon

57367652R00098